ICESLINGER

JOHN HEGENBERGER

Rough Edges Press

Iceslinger by John Hegenberger
Copyright © 2016 by John Hegenberger
Cover Design by Livia Reasoner
Rough Edges Press
www.roughedgespress.com

Rough Edges Press

ISBN-13: 978-1533020185

ISBN-10: 1533020183

All rights reserved.

This is a work of fiction. The characters, incidents, and dialogues are products of the author's imagination and are not to be construed as real.

No part of this book may be used or reproduced in any manner whatsoever without written permission of the publisher, except in the case of brief quotations embodied in critical articles and reviews.

Dedication

To the Killer Bees: Brin, Benford, and Bear

This is how my SF world began with a bang, not a whimper.

Table of Contents

ICESLINGER 1

SAVING TIME 43

NECROMANCER 63

TAMERA'S ENGAGEMENT 73

UNHAPPY TRAILS 95

THE BORIS KILLOFF 115

ICESLINGER

1

Someone in Winner Corp was trying to ruin Ted Clamber's career. Or at least it seemed that way to him.

First he'd been ordered to drop everything and catch the Io-Ganymede shuttle, with no indication of the trip's purpose. Then for two days, he floated around doing diddly, waiting for Field VP Charles Quiller to set up a meeting to explain why Ted had been pulled away from his tug assignment.

The face-off was scheduled for 16:00 in the Captain's quarters away from the passengers, crew, and cargo of the Inter-Jovian transport. But Ted would have gladly met the man at the center of the shuttle's forward radio dish, if it meant finding out why he'd been sent without warning to one of Winner Corp's Ganymede ice stations.

An amber light glowed outside the Captain's portal, signaling privacy. Ted keyed in his ID number and waited for clearance. Even this minor security delay grated on his nerves; who did they think they were dealing with? He'd been with the Corp for almost eight years now, six of them beyond the Belt. Didn't that command some sort of trust and respect? The light went green and the hatch automatically undogged.

The Captain's quarters were decorated with light wood paneling. It was a sign of status within the company, when an exec had natural Earth tones in his living space. Ted was impressed, but quickly decided that when his time came, he'd opt for something a little less gaudy than knotty pine. Maybe thick slabs of marble. The sheer cost of lifting them out of Earth's g-well ought to impress anyone.

"Thank you, Captain. We'll only need your office for a few minutes," said a rugged, blond man.

Ted waited while the disgruntled and whisker-faced officer floated out of the room. After the hatch had re-dogged itself, the blond man stuck out a hand and said, "Sorry for all the mystery, but it's absolutely necessary. I'm Chuck Quiller."

"We've met before, sir," Ted Clamber said, completing the handshake and looking directly into the man's cold, blue eyes. "Two years ago, at the company's annual meeting on Titan. I flew you and several other VPs to the Satfive station."

The older man's face remained stiff, as he

held himself in place beside the hatch. "Is that right? Well, it's a small system..."

Ted finished the familiar, Winner Corp slogan with a smile, "...and a big deal."

They both chuckled.

What a dork, Ted thought. "So what's the situation here? I was due for some downtime, when I got ordered to grab this shuttle and accompany you to Gany."

Quiller gestured toward a flatscreen embedded in the pine paneling and the two men strapped into slings in front of its keyboard. A classified personnel file was on the screen. It was Ted's.

"I don't particularly like what I read here," Quiller said. "But the CEO wants me to work with you."

Well, excuse me all to hell, old man.

"Says here that you've had almost two hundred flight hours in an Io Hopscotch. That right?"

Ted was a little miffed that his file had been accessed without his knowledge, but he knew enough to keep his mouth shut about it, for now. Besides, you don't get answers if you're busy complaining. There would be plenty of time later to pitch a bitch to Personnel about this invasion of his privacy.

"Yes," he said evenly. "I started out flying

one of those pogos when I was first assigned to the Inter-Jovian system. But why's that important? Gany's mass/density irregularities have always defeated the ship's landing computers and made it too dangerous to use a Hopscotch there."

The VP scratched his left earlobe with his right hand. "That's true enough," he said. "Until now."

Ted glowed inwardly. *Bingo. Front row.* "So, I get to pilot—"

"Not just yet," the older man told him. "You're the co-pilot...if we can manage to get the ship down to that ice ball in one piece."

Chuck Quiller downloaded Ted's file into a data chip. Then he broke the chip into slivers, destroying the info. "Last night, someone entered the cargo bay and tried to discover what was in the pogo's crate."

Ted took a guess. "Someone? You mean Tiamat? They'd love to get ahead of us in ice processing; they've only got half as many stations on Gany as Winner Corp."

"I'm certain it was someone on board who thinks Tiamat would pay plenty for info on what we're doing, or planning to do, on Ganymede. The only reason I'm not sure, is that the shuttle's DNA tracer is broken and there's no way to identify who tried to sneak a peek at our cargo."

"Well, I'll keep my eyes open," Ted said.

"You'll do better than that," Quiller told him. "Starting right now, you're standing watch over that crate until we dock at Philusulca."

Ted cursed to himself. The cargo bay wasn't heated, so he'd have to wear a stiff and clumsy pressure suit. *What a corporation. They're paying me 200 credits a day to babysit a crate.*

"Do you have a problem with my instructions?" Quiller asked, watching him keenly.

"No, Sir."

Shit runs downhill. Except in mircograv and corporations where it's all around you.

2

Ted only stood three hours watch in the cargo hold, because some mysterious person or persons upped the ante by sabotaging the shuttle's retros. The first Ted knew of it was via a comlink from Quiller telling him to trade places with him and come forward to inspect the ship's guidance system.

Quiller briefed him further as they swapped stations. The older man confided that he was beginning to suspect the Captain, except that without retros, the shuttle was helpless to ever land safely, and that no captain would be likely to cripple his own ship. Ted was instructed to lend his expertise to determine if there was any hope in repairing the command system.

Of course, it had been a thorough rip job. The computer's guts were strung out and plucked clean like harvest time in a hydroponics farm. And the backup module was missing! Ted figured the officers and security personnel would be on report for the rest of their careers.

The only thing they could do was to use the attitude adjusters as best they could to heave to and brake their glide, until another shuttle could deliver a replacement command mod. That would take days, and the Tiamat saboteur would get plenty of chances to check out the cargo.

Ted rushed back to where Quiller was guarding the goods and discovered that the VP had taken things into his own hands.

"War is hell," Quiller said. "Especially Corp War. No sense waiting for them to make the next move." He finished unfolding the Hopscotch's crate. "Come on. Get in. We'll use this baby to nudge the shuttle into a better flight plan."

Ted felt excitement and elation. No wonder this guy was a VP; he took action! And the ship was a beauty; much more elegant than the pogos he'd flown on Io.

As he climbed into the aft seat, facing the opposite direction from the pilot, Ted noticed that the ship's fuel capacity was three times that of the older models. And there were four major screens to watch as the computer calculated the grav-to-thrust ratio. This was one hot Hopscotch and he told Quiller so.

"Glad you like it, son," the VP said, initiating launch. "Our 'friends' at Tiamat will probably shit when they see it. At least I hope so. Now, if you're ready, I'll pop the bay doors and we'll see what this thing can do."

They drifted smoothly from the shuttle bay and followed the pogo's computer commands to fire the plasma engines and begin the nudging operation.

Above his head, Ted got his first good view of the approaching Jovian moon. Ganymede sat in a bowl of stars eclipsed slightly by the boiling orange and white ball of Jupiter. The dark blemish of Galileo Regio dominated the moon's surface, and the "stretch marks" of the glacier flows crisscrossed the wrinkled areas not in the primary's shadow.

The radio barked. "Mr. Quiller, this is the Shuttle Captain. Philusulca just sent up a message that another shuttle will be coming up in about a day."

"Roger, Captain," Quiller answered sarcastically. "We'll be happy to hang around long enough for your passengers and crew to get a good look at us, but then we're going to use this here fancy ship to make our own way down. If you don't mind."

Ted keyed the ship's radio and asked, "Don't you think that's a little abrupt?"

"It's damn suspicious," Quiller answered, "that a rescue message didn't come through until after this ship was launched and exposed. The last thing we need right now is a second shuttle-load of sneaking Tiamat spies. Do you have a problem with that?"

"No, sir," Ted responded. "I just don't want anyone to think we're being reckless with Winner Corp property."

"We need a shakedown cruise, anyway," Quiller radioed. "We'll be heading for Icestation Five near Aquarius Sulcus. Let me know, Clamber, if you have any trouble understanding how this baby operates."

"No problem, sir," Ted answered. *I could fly this thing with my eyes closed.* But the truth was, most of the instrument panel was new to him. And he was uneasy about the way Quiller had hurriedly decided to pull them out of the tricky situation on the shuttle. We could have damaged the ship, he thought. This guy takes too many chances. Working with him could jeopardize my career. Not to mention my life.

3

There was another tricky situation forming in front of them.

The skill of flying a pogo back on Io depended largely on the on-board computer's ability to estimate the acceleration vs. counter-thrust requirements for the short quick transport hops from site to site across the planet. Ganymede's irregular density had always played havoc with the computer's programmed estimates, making such a ship terribly expensive to operate and a threat to its occupants or the ground crew.

The two competing Corps were forced to depend on the much slower but safer ground transportation in order to get equipment, supplies, and people to and from their profitable iceslinger stations. But Winner Corp's profits would rise and eventually they would be able to buy out the Tiamat consortium, if this new Hopscotch could process the irregular data quickly enough to permit safe and efficient take-offs and landings.

Ted wanted his name to be at the top of the list, when promotions were being handed out for this new corporate triumph. But right now, his name would be sludge, if they didn't get through the ice storm they'd encountered on the way down to Gany.

He tried to contact the station, but all he got was an earful of static. "What's wrong with the radio?" he asked with alarm.

"Iceslinger Five is up near the pole, so there's heavy ion interference from Jupiter," Quiller told him. "Messes up the compass, too."

Ted felt his shorts tightening. "How the hell are we supposed to navigate in a storm like this?"

"We go in low and spot a mountain and then compare our altimeter reading with the geo-charts on your upper-left-hand screen."

"Are you nuts?" Ted shouted. "We're doing six-hundred klicks an hour. What if we hit one of those damn mountains?"

"You're the co-pilot," Quiller told him. "It's your job to navigate around them."

Screw me! Ted thought, watching a huge dark shape loom out of the swirling whiteness just off their starboard wingtip. "Where'd all this soup come from, anyway? I thought Gany was too small to maintain an atmosphere."

"It's a side-effect of our Nuclear Summer program. We heat up sections of the planetoid to facilitate the ice-mining operations. As a result, we get a little wind and fog."

"A little?" Ted growled between his teeth. "This is a blinding snowstorm!"

"Quit complaining and find us a coordinate, son. Nobody figured we'd be flying this far when they loaded the Hopscotch into the shuttle. We've only got a quarter of our normal fuel load and that's just about spent,"

"Holy shit!" Ted tried to spot a mountain top, using one eye, while he scanned the coordinates on the ship's screen with the other.

He spotted a humpbacked peek off to their left. Quiller nearly racked them up going over it, bucking the pale haze that streaked the canopy. The altimeter read six hundred meters. They were hugging the ground blind!

Ted frantically scrolled through the terrain maps for areas around Station Five. He located two possibles and keyed them into Quiller's screens.

"Try one of these," he said, praying that the whiteness would dissipate near their landing site. "They're sure to have some sort of lights down there for us to zero in on."

"Not if they don't know we're coming," the pilot said.

The static! Ted thought. We don't have a radio, so nobody down there knew that Quiller pulled the pogo off the shuttle. They were flying unannounced into the station. *When we get down, I'm going to kill this guy!*

They circled the area indicated on Ted's first screen and came up with nothing. If there was any life below them, Ted couldn't see it. The other possible site was thirty klicks to the northeast on the other side of Cadmus Tooth Mountain.

The Hopscotch shuddered as its fuel diminished.

"Are we going to make it?" Ted shouted.

"No problem," Quiller answered. "We'll forge up one side of the mountain and coast down the other, right into the IC5."

Ted was confused. "You...you know where we are?"

"I do now," Quiller answered. "Been here seven times in the last year."

You could have told me. Ted felt the pogo's vibrations fade away and his blood begin to flow again, as they eased their ship over the mountain top.

"That's the last of our fuel," Quiller said.

Below, in the distance, twin rings of laser spots shot up from the white-on-white surface. Ted was sure that the VP was approaching at a poor angle and they would skid across the ice flow and pile up on a ragged cliff. Then, he was sure that the ship would slam into the complex of domes clustered at the end of the station's accelerator, but Quiller seemed to be handling the retros as if he were conducting a casual demo, rather than risking their lives. Finally, after an abrupt scrotum-shrinking landing, they were down in one piece and Ted was sure he would have kissed the ground, if only it had been safe to take his helmet off.

"Welcome to IC5," Quiller said. "Check this baby into the inspection hanger. I'm heading for the exec lounge."

4

He'd report him, that's what he'd do! He'd take it all the way up to the CEO. The son of a bitch would lose his seniority, for pulling such a—

"Ted," someone called, as they marched along beside the frozen rails of the iceslinger leading to the loading dome. "Ted Clamber. Is that you?"

He must be hearing things. "Janny...?" he called in wonderment.

"Hey, Photon Man!"

Ted grimaced when he read the name stenciled on the helmet. That was Janice, all right. Nobody else knew him by that silly sexual reference. He turned and saw a dark bundle bounding in his direction.

"Janice Cleveburg," he called, as she caught

her momentum and clutched at his sleeve. "What are you doing here?"

"I'm the Head of the IC5 Transport Division. I thought that was you coming out of the new pogo. Pretty fancy...for a truck driver."

The faceplate of her suit was scored from months of flying grit. He could almost see the sparkle in her dark brown eyes and the hint of a smirk at the corners of her wide mouth.

"Hey, nothing to it," he lied. "I just dropped in for a cup of your lye tea."

"That's lime tea," she corrected. "Well, come on inside. I'll see what I can do. Your friend want a cup, too?"

Ted realized that Quiller had ignored them and was now entering the dome complex without him. "I don't think so, Janny," he said. "In fact, I'd just as soon keep away from that guy for a while. We've already spent too much time together."

She shrugged, linking an arm through his.

Over the next few days, Janice Cleveburg instructed Ted in a variety of Iceslinger operations. The long catapult accelerator flung loads of frozen ice up into orbital collection points outside the moon's g-well. It was one of five such stations operated by Winner Corp at leased sites on Gany's surface. The company was building a sixth station near Sicyon

Sulcus, where all the current crop of Grounddiggers were squatting.

Ted's parents had been Grounddiggers on Io. He never wanted to go back to a life of living in your truck and scooping out a claim, so some larger company could pay you a pittance for your load while making millions once it was delivered to the dryer planets, like Venus or Mars.

"I heard about your run in with Tiamat," Janice said as they walked inside the East sector of the complex. "We've had trouble with them down here, too."

"What kind of trouble?"

She shrugged and tossed her silky brown hair in a low-g swirl. She did that a lot, so she must have known how it affected him. "Missing equipment. Threats to our digger families. Just a general nuisance really, but I've heard that they're not above a little clandestine terrorism."

"Hmm," Ted mused. "Quiller calls it a Corp War."

"I'll bet they'd love to get their hands on your new Hopscotch," Janice said.

A digger truck approached the entrance, churning its way through the crushed, powdery ice. Janice checked with the driver and tested the load to evaluate its quality, while Ted scanned to help ensure there was no foreign content. Finally, the vehicle was cleared to chug along to the main scoop.

Ted watched as Janice entered the delivery into the Slinger's data system. "Having that ship for quick jumps from station to station will do a lot of good for the Transport Division." She turned her chair around and leaned her elbows against the console. The pose accentuated her modest breasts. "I'll probably get a bigger budget and two new people on staff, just to coordinate the increase in traffic. But I thought you were supposed to be test flying it with your buddy, the VP."

Ted reached out and pulled her in his arms. "I will be," he said. "Just as soon as Quiller gets through playing around." He couldn't tell her that the pogo had registered an unidentified radar source originating from somewhere between Stations Three and Five. And that, until a careful ground search could locate what was surely a hidden Tiamat operation, Quiller kept all the flights over the suspicious area to himself.

He looked deeply into her dark eyes. "Speaking of playing around..."

"Hey, Icy," the radio crackled from the console. "This is the Marker family. We need your help!"

Janice slid back into her chair and keyed a

switch on the radio. "Roger, Marker. This is IC5. You're not coming in very clear. What's the problem?" She turned and told Ted, "They're one of our diggers; probably needs a battery jump."

The voice in the radio sounded shattered. "We broke a track and one of my boys cut his hand real bad bringing it inside for repairs."

Janice scanned a printout from the vectorlink. "Is he all right?"

"Yes and no, IC5. He was inside the groundcar when it happened, so there wasn't any depressurization, but he's bled all over, so I think it's arterial."

"Roger, Marker. We have your location. Hang on; we'll have a crew and doctor out to you in about an hour. Standard rates."

"Thanks, Icy. We'll be waiting."

Janice's chair creaked as she came to her feet. "Well, Photon Man, how about a little exercise?"

"Sounds good to me, Janny. But shouldn't we do something to help that guy first?"

"Idiot! Go down to the ground crew station at the South entrance and make sure they have the coordinates." She handed him the printout. "I'll get a doctor and meet you there."

Twenty minutes later they were riding the half-track "alligator" through the rough and frozen terrain to where the Marker family waited in their crippled digger.

Ted kept his eye out for any unexpected outcroppings or gullies. Gany was known for its sinewy ridges and wavy rows of multi-layered ice.

Janice drove, while Bill Thompson, the doctor, relayed first-aid through the radio. The wind whipped around in front of them and pounded at the sides of the half-track as it slowly crunched along to the rescue site. Ted could see why the radio transmissions had been blurred. This was the harshest environment outside of the Red Spot.

When they arrived, he suited up and went out to help Papa Marker and his boys wrestle the track back onto their digger during a driving storm. The cut on young Timmy's hand proved to be deep and jagged. Doc Thompson decided to stay with his patient during the drive back, in case symptoms of shock developed.

Ted clumsily piled back into the alligator, and discovered he was drenched with sweat and feeling uncomfortably drained. "Damned suit's got a faulty AC unit," he complained aloud. "I thought I was going to drown before I could get it off."

Janice laughed and muttered something

about "the first man to drown in his own perspiration," and then steered the half-track around on a course back to IC5. "Too bad Doc Thompson isn't still with us," she said. "He's a pretty good micro-mechanic, too."

Ted was pulling his leg out of a boot when the radio spat a message at them.

"Mayday, Mayday! This is Quiller in the screaming Hopscotch. I've got a faulty fuel adjuster and am going to try and ditch into a snowbank. Coordinates 220 degrees east, 50 degrees south. Mayday!"

"That's your VP," Janice said, trying to adjust the radio while steering the half-track over the ice.

Ted came forward in the cramped vehicle and said, "Here, let me do that." He struggled to keep the signal clear, but it faded in and out and weakened completely after only a few minutes.

"The damn ion storm's starting up again. He's only about thirty-five klicks to our southwest," Janice said. "Do you want to try and catch him?"

"Hell, yes. The way he sounded, we may be the only people to have heard his message."

Janice radioed over to the Markers that they were going to break off and pursue another rescue. She told them to continue on in to IC5 and to let the security department know about the situation.

"You realize, of course," she said, swinging the vehicle around an outcropping of black rock and into the blinding wind, "that this has all the makings of a classic ambush."

Ted smiled. "Nah, it's Quiller, all right; he used the codeword, 'screaming'. I can't wait to see his face when he finds out who's coming to rescue him."

"Don't get cocky, Teddy," Janice warned. "Quiller's signal went out on a broad beam from an uncharted sector. If any Tiamat personnel picked it up, we may have a tug-o'-war on our hands."

5

They crawled along the frozen terrain for more than four hours. Ted tried to raise a response from Quiller on the radio, but the swell of Jovian ions continued to loop through the magnetosphere and blanket the frequencies. If there had been a UHF up-link in the Hopscotch, he thought, a clear signal could be received on the flatscreen. You'd think the designers would have prepared for such a situation. Ah, but that's why he and Quiller were getting haz-duty pay; it was their job to identify all the bugs before Winner Corp built a whole fleet of Hopscotches.

"I think I see something," Janice said.

Ted leaned into the forward window.

"Careful!" the woman cried, pulling at his collar. "If your face touches that frozen plex, I'll have to peel you off." Ted backed away, still trying to spot the pogo. "All I see is a deep crevasse," he complained.

"Look over to the left, on the other side. There!"

"Oh, yeah...I see it now. It's half buried in the snow."

"If we don't get over there soon, it'll be completely buried."

"Well, what are we waiting for? Let's go!"

"I suppose you noticed that canyon in front of us," Janice replied.

They had come to the edge of one of the planetoid's huge series of parallel wrinkles, one of the strange surface structures created by Jupiter's tidal forces on the Gany ice flows. It looked to Ted as if the first steep drop was at least a hundred meters straight down. And the next ridge over, where the pogo sat, was more than four klicks away.

"Doesn't look good," Janice sighed. "Your partner could be badly hurt or frozen. I'll have to find a way around this, before we pick him up."

"How long will that take?" Ted asked, hearing the edge in his voice.

"I told you this area was uncharted. I've got sky maps for general reference, but they won't tell me a thing about how safe it is to drive this hulking half-track across an ice ridge. This is one of those situations, Ted, where we're near enough to see, but too far away to help."

"Don't say that," Ted snapped. "There's a man out there possibly dying, and a classified lander worth billions of dollars. There's got to be a way to get to him. You people couldn't continue to live in this environment, if you gave up so easily. Now, what's the answer?"

Janice stroked the soft hair behind her left ear. "Well...you're not going to like it."

"Tell me."

"You could try and fit into my suit and take a jet pack over the crevasse. The winds look traitorous, but if you carried a second pack over to your VP, the two of you could shoot back here in less than an hour."

Ted swallowed dryly. His mind scrambled for another solution; any other solution. But he couldn't come up with one.

"Makes sense," he had to admit. After all, he was the pilot and she was the most experienced at driving the half-track. If anything further went wrong, she could still try and find a way across the canyon. "So, where are these jet packs?"

"Back in the locker," Janice said. "The one marked 'Danger: Explosives'."

6

I must be out of my frigging mind. Ted climbed out of the Alligator. The wind nearly took him off his feet as he strapped the jets into place on his back. Then, he radioed to Janice, "Can you still hear me?"

"Loud and clear," she responded.

The frigid wind peppered him with a frozen grit of ice. Outside his suit, the temperature was below 150 degrees and the icy wind blew past at thirty kph.

Ted stooped to pick up the jet pack that Quiller would need to get back to the alligator. The joints of his suit were already stiffening. *I'd better not stand around here much longer, or I'll become part of the scenery.*

He picked up his right foot and carefully watched the snowshoe settle on the surface of the cold, blank carpet that lead to the edge of the crevasse. "Okay," he radioed. "I'm on my way."

"Don't go too close to the edge. The ice might break off and—"

"Listen, Janny, I know what I'm doing," he

lied. "Let me concentrate, will you?"

"Just be careful, Ted."

"Keep quiet, and I will," he complained.

Flying a jet pack through this storm was going to be a real treat. Ted tromped his way to the canyon and checked the controls one more time. He calculated that a low blast would lift him up a couple of meters and then an increase in lateral thrust would carry him across the black and jagged gap in front of him. The biggest challenge, as always, would be landing. If he throttled into the wind, he could try and stay on a stationary course. And if he throttled the jet exhaust back carefully enough, he could dangle within a few meters of the downed pogo.

At the last second, he decided to switch the extra jet pack to his left arm, in order to have additional ballast against the wind. Then, he jabbed the ignition switch with his thumb and felt the jets kick him off the ground.

Immediately, he was taken by a gut-wrenching fear as the storm tried to spin him around. In another second, the wind would have him wobbling like a top. Where are the damn stabilizers on this thing? he screamed to himself, while clutching at every control he could find. His body pitched forward and, for a terrifying second, he thought he would rocket headfirst into the maw the crevasse. Steady torqueing of the left steering rod brought him upright again and the spinning was now under control, as well.

Well now, he thought, that wasn't so bad. But, why didn't I test this damn thing out, before attempting to fly across the canyon with it? He muttered into the radio, "I must have a death wish."

"You're doing fine," Janice answered. "Just don't drop the other pack."

Ted glanced down and saw that the extra jet pack was dangling from only one strap. No wonder I'm off balance, he thought, as the opposite lip of the frozen crevasse passed beneath his feet. He hefted the pack into his arms and steered a course straight for the Hopscotch.

He was throttling down and trying to catch a glimpse of any life-signs in the broken pogo, when his feet struck the slippery surface and zipped out from under him on the hard, angled ice. Fear leapt from his mouth as he went down with a crunching crack.

The wind blew white dust across his faceplate. Three red alarm lights flashed inside his helmet. He had taken Janice's suit, because the AC unit in his was faulty. Now hers had a leaking joint in the right knee, a cracked air exchanger, and a break in the radio antenna.

"Janny, can you still hear me?" he called.

"Increase the gain," came the faint reply. "Your signal's dropping."

"Shit," he said flatly.

"Come again? I can't hear you?"

"My jets melted a sheet of ice and I slipped on it. Now, my suit's all banged up!"

"Are you all right?"

"I don't know," he said, coming to his feet. "I think so, but sonofagodamnbitch!"

"What?"

"I crushed the exhaust on my godamn jet pack! You're going to have to find a way around here to pick us up. I won't be able to get this thing fixed without a godamn fucking machine shop!"

"All—all right. Take it easy. Is Quiller okay?"

Oh yeah...Ted thought. I forgot about the VP.

"Hold on. I'm going to see if I can get into the lander."

He stumbled his way over to the downed pogo and started scooping ice crystals away from the ship's hatch. He could feel a faint pounding in his palm coming from inside the Hopscotch.

"Quiller, is that you?" he radioed and then realized how stupid it must sound. Of course, it was him. "It's me, Clamber. Can you hear me?"

The hatch popped open a crack and Ted got his fingers under it, heaving upwards. From inside, a suited figure grabbed at his arms and pulled him forward.

Ted found his helmet being pressed tight against the plex faceplate of Quiller's suit. He shook his head to help adjust to the extreme close-up view of the other man's features through his own faceplate. A buzzing voice said, "My radio's down. Only way we can talk is through conduction."

Great. I can't fly and you can't talk. "Are you all right?" Ted shouted.

Quiller banged his helmet against Ted's in a nodding gesture.

Ted relayed the info to Janice. "I've got him, and he's okay. The storm seems to be dying down, so you better start coming around."

"Roger," Janice answered. "I'm heading west. If you two can walk parallel on your side of the sulca, we'll met that much sooner."

"Good idea," Ted responded, unstrapping the broken jet pack. He pulled the extra one on in its place and then conked helmets again with Quiller. "Come on, sir. We're going for a little walk."

7

They had gotten a good two and a half klicks west of the Hopscotch when the storm rose up again.

Quiller was dressed only in his flight-suit and had a hard time walking without snowshoes, but the high winds had hardened the crust into semi-solid patches, so he only sank once in the dry, sifting crystals. Ted's mind flashed on an image of them both sinking over their heads, swimming in a sea of frozen ice and methane.

The VP pulled Ted to him and said, "We're going to get lost out here in this storm. The only shelter is in the pogo."

Ted's blood seemed to thicken with fear. Quiller was right. They were going to have to go back.

An hour later, Ted was almost blind with exhaustion. The injured knee joint had frozen solid, and the air exchanger was making a threatening sound.

The storm came back in full force by the time they reached the ship. Janice and the alligator must have been out of range of his radio, because there were no responses to his many calls.

As the two men climbed back into the pogo,

Ted's stomach began to growl. *Right now, I'd give my right nut for just a whiff of Lime Tea.*

Quiller shook his shoulder and pointed.

At first, Ted didn't see anything except the Hopscotch's instrument panel. Then it hit him; one of the screens had been smashed and the fuel control programs were missing from the computer.

"I didn't do that," Quiller's voice buzzed. "We've had company."

Tiamat!

"I guess the crash and the rescue affected my judgment," the VP explained. "I should have destroyed the ship before we left."

"It's only been a few hours, at best," Ted shouted. "They couldn't have gotten very far. Let's look around."

Ted and Quiller scrambled back outside to find that the storm was letting up again.

"This damned moon," Ted cursed. He looked up. The storm seemed to have risen above them somehow. Now you couldn't even see the russet orb of Jupiter. He scrolled through the frequencies on his radio for the hundredth time, hoping to pick up a random signal from the competition.

Nothing.

Quiller was climbing up on top of a large outcropping of black rock. He waved his hands and pointed just as Ted received a faint call on the radio from Janice.

"...are you guys? Come in, Ted. Can you hear me? This is Cleveburg. I've made it around the crevasse. Where are you guys? Come in, Ted. Can you—"

"Janny! Get over here as quick as you can!"

"What—what's wrong? Are you hurt?"

"Tiamat's been in the Hopscotch and they've taken the fuel control system."

8

Janice drew up a few seconds after Quiller came down from the rock. The three of them swapped stories inside the alligator.

"We've got a good chance of stopping them, if we hurry," Quiller said. "I could see their half-track chugging along to the west."

Ted thought this was a grave risk, but he had to hand it to the VP for proposing a courageous response. "We'll have to run at top speed to overtake them. And we don't have any weapons on board, if they decide to put up a fight."

"Look, all we need to do is stop them until one of our rescue teams arrive. That shouldn't be too hard; in fact, I think I know a way that should work nicely." Quiller turned to Janice and asked, "Can you get moving?"

She looked at Ted, but answered with a nod.

"Good. Get that extra jet pack, son. As soon as we can come alongside the other vehicle, I want you to toss it to me."

Ted realized what the VP had in mind, and was grateful that the more dangerous part of the plan hadn't been delegated to him.

Twenty minutes later, the Alligator was closing in on the Tiamat half-track. Ted and Quiller were riding topside as the gap between the two racing vehicles gradually closed. Their top speed through the rough and frozen terrain was less than thirty kph, but the Tiamat tractor swerved occasionally, ramming the alligator with bone-jarring impacts.

Ted watched as Quiller timed his jump from one vehicle to the other, and then held his breath when the man landed on the Tiamat halftrack, nearly sliding along the side into the grinding treads. For a heartbeat, he hung there, his legs threatening to be ground to pulp by the whirling gears. Then the vehicle swerved away, and Quiller swung his body up from danger.

Achieving a safe perch on the top of the tractor, the VP gestured with a sweep of his hand. Ted gathered his feet under him, pulled his arm back and threw the jet pack across the gap between the two speeding vehicles. He watched as it landed heavily against Quiller's right shoulder. It tumbled and rolled, and Ted was sure it would bounce to the ground, but the VP caught hold of one strap and drew it to him.

Janice let the alligator drop back when she saw Quiller strapping the jet pack to the side of the Tiamat vehicle. Ted watched and waited while the VP and the tractor grew smaller in the distance. *Come on,* he thought. Then he moaned. Someone was crawling out of the pressure hatch on the side of the Tiamat vehicle. They had finally figured out what was going on and were coming to investigate. If Quiller didn't hurry—

The jet pack flashed to life with a brilliant glare. Quiller and the other man were thrown free, as the vehicle responded suddenly to the lateral force and skidded along the icy surface. Janice accelerated the alligator forward in a rescue attempt, as the Tiamat tractor began to spin clockwise like a roman candle, bouncing from outcropping to black boulder, until it carne to rest at a slant against a solid cliff face.

Ted launched himself at his adversary, finding an easy victory, since the man had been stunned by the fall. Within minutes, the three men were standing in a group beside the wrecked vehicle.

"All right, Weston," Ted radioed on a broad beam, having read the man's name off the side of his helmet. "Open this baby up, or we'll torch it permanently."

The man's dark eyes glared with hatred, but he shrugged his arms out of Ted's hold and bent to key in a code that opened the vehicle's pressure lock. Once inside, Ted and Quiller found the vehicle's driver, bloody and unconscious where his head had struck a protrusion above the control unit. They popped the seals on their helmets and inspected the man's wound.

"He's not dead," Quiller said. "But he's lost a lot of juice." He turned to the Tiamat man. "Better get a medpack on that wound before he bleeds to death."

Ted found the pogo's missing fuel system in a shielded storage bin. "This is all the evidence we need to get your Corp booted off the moon," he said, but Weston just snickered deep in his throat.

"He knows something," Quiller said. "What's with the laugher, mister?"

The man finished bandaging his companion and turned to face them. "The rest of my people will be here any time now."

"Don't try to bluff us, shithead. You couldn't have contacted your people; the ion flare has all the radios down."

Weston smiled. "Radios, yes. Videos, no. " He cocked his head toward a small two-way vid unit connected to the tractor's instrument panel. "Smile and wave to the folks back at Tiamat. We've been using UHF for almost a year now."

"Aw hell," Quiller said. He punched a button on the Vid unit, and a small screen to the left of the camera lens popped to life. Ted saw the face of an angry, red-bearded man.

"Weston," a stern voice called. "You are ordered to take command of those people and hold them in custody, until our task force arrives in the next few minutes."

"Task force?" Ted swallowed.

"Few minutes?" Quiller said.

"Yes, Commander!" Weston answered, but Ted shoved the man away from the camera.

"We've got people on the way here, too, you know," he said. "Any attempts to attack us and Weston here will be thrown outside. Without a suit."

"Don't let them bluff you, Commander," Weston said. "I mean nothing."

Quiller smashed a fist into the man's face. Weston's head snapped back to crack against the bulkhead and he slumped to the deck.

The screen went blank. Ted felt for a pulse

in the man's throat. "He's still alive, but we'd better get the hell out of here."

9

After a brief conference—with the Vid unit completely shut down—Ted and Quiller concluded that their best bet was to try and use the Tiamat communications system to call IC5.

Quiller searched the wavelengths, finally getting through to the station, only to discover that the rescue had been delayed because of the storm. "It'll be more than an hour," he said, "before the arrival of any assistance."

"Terrific," Ted grumbled. "I risk my life to save your neck and now I'm in the middle of a damn Corp War. Hell, I'll probably get demoted for causing a confrontation, if I ever live to tell about it."

Quiller shot him a glance and said, "If you weren't so worried about your position with the company, you'd get off your butt and do something worthwhile. Do you think I got to be a VP by hiding on an Io ore tug? No, I advanced by taking chances and risking my career against the corp's potential for profits. That's what they pay you for."

Ted felt fury building inside of him. The words stung. He had seen this man risk his life recklessly and come out on top. Maybe the way to the top was to take a few risks now and then, but he hated hearing about it from a man he'd just had to rescue.

Janice's voice came over the radio and broke the tension. "Hey, you'd better get back here. We're going to have company, real soon."

Ted bent to make sure that Weston was securely tied to his seat. Quiller collected a few extra pressure suits and the pogo's computer system.

"We'd better take the vid unit, too," the VP said. "Either that, or smash it so our friend here doesn't come to and find a way to use it."

Ted disconnected the unit from its power source and pulled it from the console. In a few minutes, the two men were cycling through the Alligator's hatch, just as two new Tiamat half-tracks came churning into view along the western ridge.

One pulled up beside the damaged tractor, but the other moved in pursuit of the Winner Corp vehicle. "We're outta here," Janice cried. And the alligator lurched to the north.

In less than ten minutes, it was clear that they would never make it. The Tiamat vehicle was much more advanced in design for rapid movement through the frozen terrain than the one they'd caused to crash against the ridge.

"Here's an idea," Ted said. "Let's call IC5 and have them adjust the sling to throw a load of ice on those guys?"

Janice ignored him, but Quiller explained that a trick like that would work only if the target were in a direct line with the iceslinger.

"I was joking!" Ted exclaimed. "Don't you ever kid around to relieve a little tension?"

"The time to kid around is after we're back at IC5," the VP said. Ted watched out the forward window. "Where the hell's that storm when we need it?"

Janice said, "I can try to keep away from him by maneuvering in and out among these outcroppings, but it's only a matter of time before they catch us."

Ted felt the pressure building up inside his head. Panic was setting in. He regretted arguing with Quiller. Now word would get back about his attitude and he'd be embarrassed out of the company. When your image became tarnished at Winner Corp, you lost your polish forever.

Janice raised IC5 on the UHF unit, while Quiller began to disassemble the fuel system from the Hopscotch. "Wait a minute," Ted cried. "What will happen when word gets out that Tiamat has attacked us?"

Janice looked up. "Nothing," she said.

"Nothing?"

Janice sighed. "Tiamat will deny everything. It'll be our word against theirs."

"I wouldn't mind it so much," Quiller said, "but it'll take at least a year to get a replacement for this fuel system. The pogo can be salvaged, but this..." He looked down at the computer module in his hands and prepared to break it in half.

"Wait!" Ted pulled the system out of Quiller's grasp. "I've got an idea how we might get out of this."

10

"Come on, you assholes," Ted taunted their pursuers over the radio, while stumbling through a drift of crystalline ice. Janice and Quiller were wading through behind him. The three had abandoned the alligator minutes ago, in order to head out on foot in the direction of their rescue team.

Ted kept the chatter going, sending the signal back to the empty half-track, where it was relayed on to the Tiamat vehicle. If all went well, the competitors would waste precious time burning their way through the alligator's thick hide.

The Tiamat Commander's voice came over the radio. "Be warned, Whiners. We are right outside your vehicle and prepared to cut our way in with laser torches, if you refuse to open up."

"Any unauthorized breach of this vehicle's integrity will be grounds for trespassing. Your company will be fined heavily for claim jumping, murder, and theft. Tiamat Corp will be restricted from operating on Ganymede, when the System Regents learn the truth. So, back off, shithead." Ted wished he were as confident as he sounded. They were taking a hell of a chance with this reverse Trojan Horse bit.

If the rescue team didn't show up soon, the three of them would die from exposure as the power supplies in their suits dwindled to nothing. A quick check of his own power gauge told Ted that he had only ten minutes until his heating unit shut down for good.

The Commander's voice crackled over the staticy radio. "You poor dumb Whiners. No one will ever know that we are cutting open your vehicle. When they examine the evidence, we will say you were trapped, or killed in an accidental fall into one of the canyons."

Quiller tugged at Ted's sleeve, in order to maintain radio silence, but pointed to their right.

The Tiamat Commander's voice continued in

the radio. "According to my estimate, you will die from the heat of our torches in the next minute, Whiners. We have tried to negotiate with you, but we knew you wouldn't give up your precious fuel system without dying."

Two large alligators came around a ridge, heading for the empty half-track. Janice signaled them with a strobe, and the three companions began slogging their way to a rendezvous as Ted radioed, "This is my final warning, Commander. If you insist on attacking our vehicle, you will pay the consequences."

"We attack now, you son-of-a—"

Ted switched off the radio and continued making his way toward the arriving alligators. Quiller and Janice were the first to board. Since the lock would only cycle two people at a time, he danced from foot to foot impatiently waiting his turn. Finally the seal opened and he tumbled inside. The second that the inner seal broke, he popped his helmet and asked, "Did they buy it?"

"They sure did," Quiller answered, pointing to a vid screen. "They're coming through now."

"Wait 'til they find out they're on Vid relay up through Winner's Comsat," Janice said. "Ten minutes from now, every media transmission in the System will be carrying an instant replay of Tiamat's brutal attack on a downed Winner Corp vehicle."

"They'll never work in this town again," Ted laughed.

Quiller munched on a ration bar. "That was a damn fine idea, son. And you see what I meant about taking a risk, in order to gain success. But, we'd better get out of here. Those boys mean business."

"Not anymore," Janice said, giving Ted a squeeze.

"Thank you, sir," Ted answered. "I've been watching you and I've learned the truth of that old adage, No guts, no glory."

"Good for you," Quiller said. "When I first met you, I thought you were as cold as the iceslinger, but you warmed up nicely. When we get back, I'll see that you receive a nice promotion out of this."

"And, I'll see that you receive a nice cup of lime tea," Janice laughed.

Quiller grimaced. "How can you drink that stuff?"

(Originally appeared in *Life Among the Asteroids,* Ace Books, 1992)

SAVING TIME

I have a hard time getting up in the morning. My back feels as if a million ants with razor feet had spent the night on spine patrol. It's not the dry cough in my throat, or the pulsing beat behind my eyes. I can take physical pain; my injured wrist proves that. It's the feeling of loss, as if my life is almost over, that I had an opportunity to do things once, but now I've pissed it all away.

Karen acts as if she understands, but how can she possibly know what I go through each morning? She didn't age fifty years in a minute.

* * *

I gather up my notes and set fire to them in the soldering furnace's blackened well. The lab fills with smoke, and I remember to open the air vents letting the grey clouds dissipate over the white Wisconsin snow.

Unmindful of the pungent odor, I pluck a hammer from the workbench with a claw-like arthritic hand and beat the hell out of the black metal programming unit.

I work up quite a sweat, gasping for breath in the dense dark air. My heart beats against my scrawny ribs like a snared rabbit. I've trapped myself again.

Karen comes in and finds me among the debris. She calls me a "crazy old man." It's the worst thing she can say. I slap her full in the face, and instantly hate myself for the act.

In a rage, I slam a fist into the bracket holding the time machine's recording computer and feel the flesh tear against its sharp metal edge. The pain blinds me into unconsciousness.

* * *

The mind is the most powerful force in the universe.

Remember all those time travel stories you read as a teen? They were full of strange paradoxes and terrible twists in the end for the greedy person who discovered the future results of horse races and stock market closings. The stories were like hi-tech deals with the devil. Just when the hero thought he'd get everything he could ever wish for—suddenly, he got nothing but a trick of fate and eternal damnation.

I made certain that this would never happen to me. I had no ulterior motive for seeing the future. I just wanted to do something that had never been done before. Is it a crime to attempt the impossible? Why should I bear the fate of the trickster for wanting to advance a scientific principle?

* * *

I awake in our bed, more in pain than before, my arm in a makeshift sling.

"It's not too bad," Karen says, putting down her book. "You missed cutting the artery in your wrist." She speaks quietly, making me wonder if perhaps my hearing is going, too. "I could take you to the hospital, but they'd want to know about your health insurance."

"And we can't have them wondering about that," I say, inspecting the bandage. "I'm a non-person, now." My mouth is as brittle and dry as the ashes in the furnace.

Karen holds out a plastic cup with a straw angled in it. I sip the cool water and accept another pain pill from her open palm. My head settles down into the pillows.

"You've got to control your temper, Sam," she lectures me. I focus on the book she's reading; Gleick's *Chaos*. "You could have killed yourself in there," she gestures toward the lab with her pert chin, "or set fire to the warehouse. You know the alarms don't work."

I smile faintly. "Another failure," I muse. "Ever wonder what would have happened if I'd travelled farther than fifty years? What a failure that would have been."

"I don't want to think about it; and neither should you," she clucks, tucking the blankets beneath my chin. "You're still here and that's all that matters."

A large wetness gathers in my eyes. "The year would have been a little beyond 2040. Christ, what a way to have died. Aged in an instant." She dabs at my tears, telling me to rest.

I float off thinking that the greatest irony of old age comes when you're treated like a baby.

* * *

Since we weren't working with explosives or radioactive materials, it had seemed unnecessary to place the time machine in an enclosed space. So, there it sat in the middle of the warehouse, a simple office chair with a standard adjustable back and swivel seat. It required no elaborate control panel or steering wheel as in the movies, because we didn't expect to drive it anywhere. An IBM clone set on a table next to the programmable controller and power source, but the real brains of the device rested on the top of the spine of the subject who would sit in the chair.

The working hypothesis was based on a 1927 technical paper by Otto Veblen published in The Journal of Neurology and Psychosomatic Medicine, entitled "The Correlations of Spatial/Temporal Dimensions to Aesthetic Reference." I'd dredged the thing up from the stacks of the University of Wisconsin Psychology library, of all places.

Stated briefly, Veblen contended that there is an instant of timelessness when the mind switches from one interpretation of an optical illusion to another. During this time, the mind is completely open to the paradoxes of reality and can travel forward through the fourth dimension.

Geometrically speaking, the process worked something like this:

The point has no dimensions.

The line has one dimension: length.

The square has two dimensions: length and width.

The cube has three dimensions: length, width and height, but the mind knows that it is still seeing a two-dimensional figure on paper.

This new figure of a transparent cube has four dimensions: length, width, height and an optical illusion of existing in two directions at once. But, the mind still knows that it is seeing a two-dimensional figure.

This fourth dimension is the instant of time when the mind travels freely from one view to the other. Time then is an invisible "optical illusion." The more complex the illusions, the more the mind is conditioned to travel uninhibited—almost in anticipation—directly forward. Backward travel in time is impossible. Period. What's done is done. You can never go home again. All the paradoxes occur when you travel backward in time, not forward.

Working within Veblen's subjective elasticity of time, Karen and I constructed the central part of our machine. We scavenged an early version of an Air Force training helmet used by pilots to tele-operate an aircraft by presenting a series of convincing images through the video-display worn directly over the subject's eyes.

By reprogramming the output to the goggle's screens, we could fill the subject's brain with a billion data-bytes of multi-level illusion information. This massive subliminal burst of timelessness would build to a critical point in the subject's mind, liberating the consciousness from the present and driving it forward at an estimated rate of ten days per second.

* * *

Karen is alive with youth. Barely thirty, she moves with the grace of a child. Her auburn hair flows as if in defiance of gravity. It floats and gathers around her head in a pillow of soft russet curls. Her skin is smooth and quick to flush when I get her mad. Her eyes still smile out at me, reminding me of how I once held her attention. But now they hint at accusation, as does her mouth, and at times even her stance.

I'd be only a year her senior, if I hadn't been so hasty. Some people go through a second childhood; I'm going through a second identity crisis.

* * *

"Did you read this article on hi-temp supercon?"

"Hmm?" I'd answer, trying to get a clear wave on the scope.

She'd push the journal in my direction with both hands. "Listen to me, Sam. I think this is important. This article. It says they've succeeded in achieving superconductivity for a nano-sec at room temperatures."

I'd switch off the scope, letting the green wave fade back into nothingness and take the proffered technical journal. "How do you find all these things?" I'd ask. "I leafed through this last night and didn't see—"

"That's the trouble with you," she'd say. "You leaf through everything."

I'd grunt and scan the article.

"Haven't you ever heard anyone say to take time to smell the roses?"

I'd look up, genuinely confused. "What do I care about roses?"

It never seemed to matter to Karen if I were a little absent-minded. She expected that and helped me along with the mundane things in life. Except in bed, of course. There I'd act my age. A young bull who had her full attention. All my work and frustration would dissolve away like sugar in a spring shower, and I'd take her slowly and bittersweetly, the way she wanted me to, even then.

I was sure that Karen had been drawn to me because I represented to her a doorway to the realm of pure science. She would lock minds with me and we would soar into the strata of hyper-theory, always believing that what we supposed, what we invented, could, with enough faith and willpower, become a reality. Like children, we were never fearful of the results or consequences. Blind, innocent youth.

* * *

I used to think I was happier then. When Karen and I first formulated the underlying principle of Veblen's theory, we were caught up in a dizzy dance of data and conjecture. It never bothered me that we couldn't invade the past. That was somehow satisfying and reasonable. Who cares about the past anyway, I thought. We're buried in a sea of historical reference. We live so much in the past that it holds us down so that we can barely imagine the future. Anyone who's lived has explored a piece of the past.

Faintly, I recalled growing up during the Cold War; the initial scientific drive to beat the Soviets to the moon. The Viet Nam war had spurred the development of weapons technology. The Pill and AIDS had changed the country's social structure. Genetic engineering. Superconductors, Chaos and mini-computers all conspired to accelerate the growth of scientific knowledge during my lifetime. But that was all part of the past and the present. What I didn't know, what nobody knew, was what would happen in the future!

I felt as if I were standing at the edge of a frontier! The thrill of the hunt tasted like fresh blood in my mouth. There was an uncharted, almost mystical, area of science ahead of us all, and I was determined to achieve a scientific satori, of sorts.

* * *

I work up a healthy sweat, barking the skin of my fingers on the painted steel brace that would hold the recording computer in place next to the mini-step transformer. It had fit together perfectly before I'd broken it and sliced my wrist in the same stupid rage.

I struggle with a vise-grip, crimping the sharp metal brackets into their former shape and place. The wrong tool for the right job. What I want is a solid iron hammer to blacksmith the damn things, but that's how I'd gotten into this mess the first place. The right tool for the wrong job.

My knees cramp again, so I shift my weight. Karen comes over to squat next to me.

"Can I help?"

I hand her the clattering vise-grip and get dizzily to my feet.

"I didn't mean you had to quit," she sighs, watching me walk toward the bedroom. We are both dismayed, I realize, but for different reasons.

"I'm trying to avoid an argument," I assure her, massaging my right knee. "I need a break. Call me when you've had enough."

She studies the bent and paint-chipped brackets. listen to the clicking of the grips as I lay on the cool, dark bed.

* * *

Something they never teach you in grad

school is the value of patience. The academic world pushes you forward, always wanting you to publish more papers, write more grant proposals, hurry up and affect some results. But you're a tyro, a young turk, recklessly ready to tackle anything and to show the world how brilliant you are.

So you rush about seeking grand results, skipping steps, not because you're eager to cheat, but because your colleagues would never discover your lameness. I was afraid that if I dwelt too long on any part of the experiment, the whole thing would die on me, or worse yet I'd get lost in the maze of detail. So, I forced the detail forward.

It was winter break. I was living fulltime in the lab. Karen came home each night from her work at the neural research institute and we would throw ourselves into the fabrication and perfection of the device that would trick a mind into seeing the future.

Damn my youthful folly! It needed more analysis, exploration, and repetition until it became as common and boring as getting out of bed. But I wanted to impress her with my success. I wanted to save time.

How could I ever have thought that heat could take the place of light? That smoke was the same thing as fire? That I was immortal and could try the final experiment on myself?

* * *

I'm having more trouble with the machine. I never should have smashed it. My hands don't always do what I tell them. And even when I do succeed in grasping things, often times they still slip through my fingers, even when I'm concentrating.

What frightens me most is that my mind might be suffering from the same ailment. I can easily recall events that occurred fifty relevant years ago, but when I try to remember what I had for breakfast, or where I placed a pair of needle-nose pliers, it's all gone like smoke.

My glasses no longer suit my eyesight. I get fierce headaches whenever I try to read. My teeth are weakening, my back is more bent each day, my hair is falling out in brushfuls.

My liver must not be functioning properly; spots are appearing on my face and the backs of my hands. I wonder about my other vital organs. I know now that the cut on my wrist isn't going to heal properly.

* * *

I'll admit it: I took a terrible chance. But nothing of value is wrested from the universe without risk. "You've got to gamble a little to gain a lot," I'd tell Karen.

I remember the acrid smell of soldering iron mingled with anchovy pizza. The television displayed a constant stream of VH-1 hits.

One snowy night in January, a 40-ft. semi-truck skidded out of control on the icy freeway exit ramp and took out the power substation, crashing the entire evening's programming. I cursed, then killed a fifth of scotch.

In the morning, I awoke in a painful daze. Karen had spent the night re-entering all the lost data, before heading off to work at the institute.

I cooked her favorite dinner that night, lasagna a la Ryan, and promised never to get drunk again.

* * *

I settled into the chair. The goggled helmet rested in my lap, its bunched leads trailing to the floor and over to the CPU. Karen was due home in twenty minutes. I wanted to share the experience with her, but I also wanted to be sure it would work before involving her further. Hell, I wanted to test it myself, that's all. Plain and simple, I wanted to be the first person to see the future.

My palms were sweating. I discovered that I needed to go to the bathroom. I rubbed my eyes, the eyes that would wear the goggles, the eyes that would receive the computer's onslaught of optical illusions. I thought about the magic, the misdirection and everything else done with mirrors.

I flushed the toilet and went to the sink, running the water until it was good and cold. Karen should be arriving in ten minutes. I could wait that long, couldn't I?

I drank a paper cupful of icy Wisconsin tap water and decided to write a note, letting her know what I had done—planned to do—in case anything went wrong. After the journey, I could always tear it up and throw it in the trash. Then, she'd never know that I'd gone ahead without her.

I sat back down in the swivel chair, hearing it creak with my weight. Everything seemed so hyper-immediate. You don't set out for the future without taking full stock of the present.

I slipped the helmet over my head and adjusted the goggles to rest comfortably on my eyes. I was ready to see the future. Ready and willing. Karen would be here any minute. I groped with my right hand for the keyboard on the table beside me. I hit the Enter key twice and felt the high exhilaration of a roller-coaster passenger on the brink of the first deep plunge.

Exactly as planned, the images drove

directly into my forebrain, flipping and flopping back and forth from one interpretation to another. The pace increased and I opened my mind to seeing opposite points of view in the same instant. I caught an updowness, followed by a inoutness and a backforwardness, a highlowness, a beforeafterness, a nowthenness, a bittersweetness, an everynothingness, a nothingeveryness, a godness, a meness, a oneness, a noneness, a widewhiteopeness...

* * *

I take very small steps to avoid the pain in my joints. If I fall and break my hip or knee, it, like my wrist, will probably never heal properly.

My hands tremble occasionally. I see myself feeble, fumbling and frustrated.

I wake in the middle of the night for no good reason, unable to fall back to sleep. I doze in the big soft chair in front of the television almost every afternoon, dreaming of yesterday when I was so much younger.

The time machine I had built succeeded in fooling my mind. So, I am my own trickster, my own devil. The illusionary images freed me to accept the future. What I failed to take into account was how great the effect would be accelerated by my totally cooperative and hopeful attitude.

The mind is still the most powerful force in the universe. Positive wish fulfillment interacts with the subliminal program and increases the rate tenfold. I didn't see the future, I became it, and time is not something you travel through; it's something you collect.

"You are as old as you think," the adage claims. My brain thinks that it has amassed more than eighty years of existence, and it has forced a psychophysiological effect on my body, telling it to be an old man.

At first, there was an enormous surge in my biological clock. I took on ten years each day during the first seventy-two hours. Gradually, the aging slowed and I've leveled off as a wrinkled and bent fumbler who can hardly concentrate past his immediate future.

Karen watches me in mute fear. I wonder how much longer before she'll leave me, or I'll die.

* * *

"I'm sorry," I say.

"I know," she answers. "It doesn't matter."

"Yes, it does." I point a shaking gnarled finger at the empty air. "If I hadn't been in such a rage, the machine would still be in one piece. I hate being this helpless and I refuse to sit quietly, growing weaker and older by the day!"

"It doesn't matter, Sam," she says, taking my cold hand hers. "In many ways, you haven't changed a bit."

I laugh dryly.

She sits beside me at the computer console we've jury-rigged back together. "What are you working on now?" she asks.

I tap a few keys to put the opening sequence on-screen. "If time is something you collect," I say, "and you do it by being open to optimum input, it follows that you can lose time by going back through the same input, but acting deterministically, making clear and active decisions, avoiding options, choosing your way over and over until you've trapped yourself in a groove that will make you unaware that time is collecting."

"But you get younger from this?" she asks.

"If you control all of your decisions—leaving no 'time' for day-dreaming—time will pass, but you won't be aware of it. I want to use the computer program to accelerate the process, to become disillusioned, caught up in decision making process and unable to realize time is passing."

"It sounds like word games to me," she says. "But in a weird way, I think I see. You want to distract your thoughts away from the passage of time and hope to psychosomatically trick your body back to its original age. But travelling backward in time is impossible."

"I used to think so," I tell her, "but now I don't know. It just seems that I deserve to get back to being thirty again. Maybe shedding years that you should never have collected in the first place isn't the same as travelling backward in time. Maybe I can trick the trickster and get back to where I started. It's worth a try. Will you help me?"

"Of course."

* * *

I remember attending a performance as a child of the play *Peter Pan*. In the middle of the third act, they stopped the show and explained to the audience that Tinkerbell wouldn't die, if we all clapped our hands and believed. The audience responded by shouting and stamping their feet as well as clapping their hands until the little fairy burned bright again.

I am as determined now as I was then, alive with a resolve I haven't felt in...fifty years.

Lowering my bony body into the creaking swivel chair, I wait almost breathless as Karen adjusts the helmet on my balding pate. What was it Peter Pan used to sing? "I won't grow up. I'll never be a man?" Ha!

I feel a tingle of excitement. This is going to

work, I think. Intent on making active choices, my mind will forget all about time. I concentrate expectantly on the screens before my eyes, prepared to make a billion conscious decisions, ignoring options, clapping my hands if I have to and stamping my feet until I've trapped myself in a groove of controlled positive reality over and over, losing time, leaving the future far behind me in the past, existing only in the eternal present.

"Are you ready?" Karen asks.

There is only one word in my vocabulary. Through dry and grimly pressed lips, I say it: "NOW!"

* * *

I have a hard time getting up again this morning. My back is fine. Even the pain in my wrist is fading. It feels luxurious to lie under the warm blankets, like a kid playing hooky from school.

I open my eyes and stare at the dull grey ceiling, thinking for a moment that it had all been a dream. But then I see the dozen long-stem roses on the dresser and I know I've won my deal with the devil and will never play his game again.

I turn my head and feel no soreness, no throbbing, no stiffness in my joints. Karen is asleep beside me. The morning light plays softly on the down of her face. Her auburn hair lays fanned on the pillow.

She's stood by me when I needed her most, and I won't risk losing her again.

Her eyes open and she smiles.

I hover over her, moving my hard lean body into place with determination.

"You idiot," she laughs. "We don't have time for this; you'll be late for your first day at the institute." But she doesn't resist me.

"It's not how much time we've got that matters," I whisper, as she matches my rhythm. "It's what we do with it."

NECROMANCER

November 29

Watched the original "Invasion of the Body Snatchers" last night. Had seen it before, of course, years ago—when I was still alive.

It's the one where some alien vegetable form takes over citizens of Santa Mira, California. Silly movie. Old, too. Reminded me of a lot of those other vampire legends. People have a whole mythos about outside intelligences taking over their bodies, using things like voodoo, and stealing their freedoms. Glad I don't have to worry about those superstitions anymore.

Got enough to sweat with selling life insurance. Ever since the perfection of Necrotech, folks know that their bodies will be sold and used again after they're dead. It's not a curse; it's a business. The money from the sale goes to the survivors, so who cares about life insurance anymore? Still, that's my job: finding clients, meeting in their living rooms and explaining actuary tables. Good thing they don't know I'm a Deadman, or they'd never sign. Tough duty, but that's my programming. It's quiet, safe, and leaves me plenty of time to be with the family and watch old movies.

* * *

December 21

Went to church again. Don't know why they bother with that foolishness. When you're dead, you're dead. Strange concept: the Holy Spirit. It's invited into a person's soul. "Fill us with the Holy Spirit," they sang. Why do these things continue to bother me?

* * *

January 1

Remembered something. During downtime at night, thought of other experiences than my own. How is that possible?

Seemed as if I worked at a clinic, or biolab. Lots of controlled samples. Beakers, flasks, enhanced lymphocytes. How could I know that? Deaders aren't supposed to dream.

* * *

February 4

Vid reports. According to the news programs, the human brain slows down after ten minutes of intense observation of the vid screen. Gale and Tommy took me to the theater. Crowds of people paying to sit in a large darkened room and have their minds affected by wide, colorful images of stimulating events and rich, loud sounds. Gale said I was too analytical. Tommy thought that was a good sign.

"Don't you feel anything?" she asked.

Her eyes began to fill with tears again.

Shrugged.

Tommy took our hands and walked between us. "It'll be all right," he said. Can't remember the name of the movie, but the title ended with a number.

* * *

February 10

Drugs. Don't mind eating, but this alcohol has a blindingly painful effect on my system. Neighbor across the hall smokes tobacco. Tried it once; hurt my awareness and perception of reality.

* * *

March 6

Don't understand Gale's art. Told Gale, and she thought I meant paintings or sculptures. Don't understand *any* art. Music, dance, poetry, architecture.

Seems like mass hypnosis. Generation-fostered hoax. What purpose does it serve these people?

* * *

March 11

Didn't have all these problems when I first became a Deader. Everything was peaceful then. No worry. No guilt. Gale was upset, but she handled it well, considering. Tommy was a real trouper. He'd have made a wonderful lab tech.

Wonder why I think that? They keep telling me I worked in a lab. Even took me there one time. Seemed a little familiar, at first. Then decided it was something I'd seen on the news, or in a movie. Left me cold.

* * *

March 15

Caught Gale crying again last night. She'd been out with Norman, but had come home alone, tipsy. She called me into the bedroom and made me put my arms around her. Her eyes searched for something in my face.

Held her as she instructed. Did everything she said, but felt nothing.

She held my face in the palms of her hands. "This has to stop," she told me.

"What?"

"I need you, Andy. You've got to come back to me."

"I'm right here."

"No you're not!" she cried and pushed me away.

Sat in a chair until she fell asleep.

* * *

April 2

Getting closer to the answer. Read a book about Zen by Alan Watts: *Be Here Now*.

What is reality? Tricky business. Simple converging lines in two dimensions "suggest" a third dimension, depth, perspective. Esthetics.

If we don't know what life is, then what is death? Anti-life? Anti-atoms in my blood?

It's okay not to know all the answers; not to worry about things too much. Made me feel good, content. Refuse to worry about why a deadman can have feelings. Must move beyond all that.

* * *

May 23

Sex. Somehow my body seems to move by itself. Watched it from inside myself, but couldn't get it to follow my restrictions. Almost automatic. Who's in charge?

* * *

May 25

Sleep. Another "bodily function". Includes

dreams. Dreams; they bother me. Their power is enormous and a lot like the movies or vids... only much more secret and personal.

* * *

June 7

Gale is fed up.

"The government has paid to keep you in a home," she said, "and I can't fight it any longer. I have my own life to live. Don't you see? It's not your fault. It would have happened to us regardless of your self-treatment. Besides, it's not so bad. They use Deadmen for lots of menial tasks now. Bus driving, baby sitting, even caddying, forgodsake! You've got to get over it, Andy. Maybe the therapy will do some good."

* * *

June 8

Deadmen. Some people trade and collect them. Kids get them for Christmas now. Deadmen on Mercury. Deadmen in college, taking exams for the living. Deadmen used as memory banks. Deadmen used to beat up bullies. Deadmen in the police force. In the hospitals, monitoring patients. In the movies. On the streets, just standing there. Deadmen as a protein substitute. Deadmen as a "living" art form. Deadmen in college, giving the exams.

* * *

June 20

Undergoing therapy today.

Psychology unifies and combines most of the other mysterious elements. The lies, the sex, the dreams, the drugs, the various conflicting aspects of Reality and Truth. Having experienced quite bit of this now, I find that there are thousands of variations and opinions regarding Reality. I find that I am. I.

Must choose a Reality and then act accordingly. If I do, I'll appear to be "cured" and they will leave me alone. But I'm not insane; I'm dead! Don't they understand? I didn't cause all these Deaders to be walking around; I'm innocent.

Not so sure I want to leave this place. Didn't like selling insurance anyway. Besides, I can learn a lot about psychology, this way. The only problem is the shock therapy and the drugs. They keep giving my body things that make it uncooperative. And call me Doctor Westfield. I toy with the identity of I, Doctor Westfield.

* * *

July 12

Dying, now.

But how can this be? Am already dead, aren't I? Aren't I? How can I die, if I'm already dead? Am I not dead?

"You're not dead," they tell me. "It's all in your mind. You've suffered a withdrawal. Your guilt for having perfected the Deader fluid made you empathize with all the bodies that have been reanimated."

"Yes," I say. "It's my fault."

"No, there is no fault, Dr. Westfield. What you've done has helped mankind. You've freed us all from mindless labor. You've shown the way to eternal prosperity. Admittedly, there have been problems, but that's exactly why we need your help."

"My help?"

"Yes, we can't go on without you, Dr. Westfield. Your achievement set the standard. The economy is booming. "

"But it's all so complex. The dreams, the media, the art, the sex..."

"We'll help you. Your wife and son will help you, too. You'll be all right, Doctor. You've done a wondrous thing for mankind. You've given it a great gift. You'll see."

* * *

November 8

I know what they meant. It's difficult to deal

with life and all its confusions. I refused for a long time to accept my responsibilities. It seemed as if the Deaders had it easier than everybody else; free of guilt and doubt. But when you're dead, you're dead. I know that now.

We flew to Stockholm for the award ceremony. Gale and Tommy loved it. I felt foolish in a rented tuxedo accepting the prize. But I got a chance to meet and compare notes with several important colleagues who heralded me as a man of genius.

But I know better; I'm just a man who saw a job that needed to be done. A man who advanced the technology one step farther along its endless progression. Nothing to feel guilty or proud about. Nothing at all.

* * *

November 23

We watched another movie tonight. An ancient superstitious nonsense-thing, called *Frankenstein*.

It made me wonder if it's possible for Deadmen to achieve free will.

I plan to begin analysis on this question in the lab tomorrow morning. I have a new idea.

TAMERA'S ENGAGEMENT

The mind of Winston Clarke, such that it was, churned the data, searching for a cross-corollary MARSDAX index for a half-dozen entries in the financial net. It was dull, hard work and Winston would be glad when his shift was over and he could relax with Tamera, once again.

* * *

From high in the purplish twilight, his taxi zoomed down on the flower-ringed stucco house and made a wide turn into the semi-circular driveway. As Winston emerged, paying the fare, he gave the packet of miniaturized diamonds in his breast pocket reassuring tap.

Upon arriving at Honolulu earlier that day, Winston Clarke, known to corporate cops and criminals alike as the Bishop, had holophoned his Chinese client to confirm that the half billion dollars had been deposited in Winston's account. The exchange of the diamonds was scheduled to take place over dinner. The Bishop accepted the invitation, innocently trusting his Guardian Angel to keep him from fatal or financial harm.

The door of the stucco villa swung open as

he approached. A lizard in an oriental robe stood inside, asking for and receiving Bishop's weapon. Hissing slightly, he led Winston through the foyer, almost colliding with a heavyset, beaming Chinese, who greeted him with a ceremonious bow.

"Please excuse my impatience," the man said. "It betrays my anxiety to possess the diamonds." He made a gesture for Winston to proceed. "Dinner is waiting for us. You indicated you wished to depart as soon as possible."

The low table was meticulously set. Winston's host noticed his hesitation as he glanced around at the half dozen cushions, trying to decide which one to sit on.

"I hope you don't mind my country's customs, food and costumes." The Chinese indicated his own flowing, handsomely-decorated robe. "I had chopsticks placed next to your setting, but if you wish the usual fork and knife..."

"Not at all." The Bishop smiled. "I've enjoyed the use of your eating utensils in many of my Chinese adventures."

The host's brow wrinkled as he moved to the head of the table and descending onto the cushion like a deflating balloon. "Please excuse my impatience. It betrays my anxiety to—"

Damn it, Winston Clarke thought, we've already had that line. He complained aloud, "You've lost your place in the script again, Tamera."

The scene froze and the conversational voice of Tamera Kane seemed to fill the air. "I'm so sorry, Winston," she said. "But it's time for you to go back on line and recompute the MARSDAX index for tomorrow's trading."

He was furious. These interruptions were becoming intolerable. Struggling to remain diplomatic, he said, "Hell, Tamera, not again! Just when things get interesting, you drop me back into the data processing programs."

"Come on, Winston," Tamera sighed. "You know Mr. Simon needs those figures. It will only take a few minutes, and then I'll tell you the rest of the story."

"To hell with what Simon needs! I'm sick of being told what to do. I need some fun and relaxation." Winston decided to force the issue. "Either you continue the story, or I'll SNAP to another channel."

"My, aren't we bristly today?"

"Bristly? You're the one who scrambled the narration! I don't know why I put up—"

"Oh, stop complaining, Winston. You're acting just like an adolescent."

That did it. He knew it would hurt her, but

he didn't care. The stupid woman was messing up his fantasies. "I mean it, Tamera. It's bad enough that you make so many mistakes, now you expect me to increase my output of damn dull financial data, just to please that faceless god Simon. Well, the answer is no. I need some quality time for myself."

"You've said that for over twenty years, Winston. If you'd stop—"

"That's it, baby. I've had it. Good-bye."

SNAP.

* * *

What was she going to do with him?

Tamera Kane sighed, removed her headphones and stretched the kinks out of her spine. She had tried her best to hold him, but lately Winston Clarke was too demanding for her poor patience. All he wanted any more was a constant serving of action, adventure, and suspense. Maybe she was getting too old for him. Maybe she was getting too old, period.

She pressed fingertips to temples and sat back wearily in her seat. He'd been right about the mistakes in the script. Each day, it became more and more difficult to remember where she had taken the story. Last week she had introduced the same character twice in two days, and the week before that she had forgotten to properly establish the setting. It hadn't always been this hard.

Tamera had been a Guardian Angel for over thirty years. Day after day, she came to the Christopher Capital Building, the only structure on Mars made from the rare smooth marble mined near the permafrost, and walked down the stairs to the Vaults where Winston and all the other Frozen Folk lived, worked, and waited for their Angels to descend unto them.

At first, these inanimates had consisted of the victims of GRGA, a cell-bonding disruption that had spread nearly a century ago. Then other victims of other diseases had been added when it was discovered that the coldsleep somehow heightened the subject's mental processes. Each of the bodies in the Vault were protected from time's decay by the cold cryonic crypts, but each mind continued to function, seeking stimulus and companionship from those on the outside.

Tamera became engaged to the Vault's communications system on her fortieth birthday. Her previous life had been ordinary and a little lonely. But like any new nurse, there had been hope and a sense of purpose when she'd began her duties. A Guardian Angel was expected to serve, to guide, to teach, and to sympathize.

At first, Tamera's stories were clumsy and disjointed, but she had a natural ability to open up and share her inner-most visions, which was the hallmark of all good Guardian Angels. Soon, she was spinning yarns and interacting with her patients like a professional—which, in fact, is what she'd become.

Still, she recalled being extremely self-conscious at her first meeting with Winston. He was such a demanding audience! Like a child, he kept asking "Why?" until she felt she would scream with frustration. Finally, she channeled the emotion into one of the characters with which Winston liked to identify, a little girl who was being chased by an ugly Earthman named Winstone. He got the picture and understood that she was just as afraid of him as he was of her. They accepted each other from that day forward.

Winston became her favorite. He yearned for the exciting "reality" that she was happy to give. He strolled through the most fantastic adventures, knowing she was always there to guide him close to the mortal dangers, but to keep him away from the fatal pain. She too dreamed of the fantasyland which she had, where a person could do anything, be anyone, battle any evil and always win.

Directing the storyline, building the "reality" had become Tamera's lifework. She selected the stories for him with great care and tailored them to his taste. For the last thirty years, she had calmly and carefully created complete worlds populated by hundreds of generations of fascinating characters. This social interaction with a patient was highly preferable to loops of video adventures; it kept the mind alert and the will inspired.

In an age of skintights with velcro patchpockets and corrective eye operations, Tamera wore full-flowing skirts and plastic-rimmed glasses. Being a Tale Spinner, an Interactor, a glorious Guardian Angel for the most important mind on Mars, she could dress any way she desired. And what she desired were comfortable clothes and quiet colors. But her long blonde hair had slowly turned to grey and her greatest frustration had become that Winston still thought of himself as a spry and eager thirty-two-year-old, while she was now nearing seventy.

All day long, she sat at her formfitting chairdesk with notes at hand of the previous days' events and cross-references on computer for easy access should Winston ask one of his interminable questions about an obscure character or event from tale's past. Like all the other Guardian Angels, Tamera spoke through her headphones to the computer that linked her to Winston. She drank and ate at her station and only broke the connection when her body demanded it, or when she left for the night. Her engagement to Winston felt natural, a thing that would go on forever. But she knew her recent increase of mistakes meant that age was getting the best of her. How would she ever manage to tell him that the end was near?

* * *

The door slammed shut, the lock caught, and the yellow gas began to fill the room.

The Bishop, bound hand and foot with heavy rope, managed to wriggle his way along the floor to the small crack beneath the door. At least he would breathe for a few minutes longer.

What had the woman, Leviticus Syn, said? "You'll be dead and then I'll have full control of the military computers and nothing will stop me." Ah, yes, that Love Syn was quite a girl.

The Bishop worked at the small blade concealed in his ring. After several moments of finger contortion, he succeeded in putting a deep laceration in his bindings.

When he was at last free, the room was

completely full of deadly gas.

Winston held his breath and told himself not to panic. His Guardian Angel was still with him when he inserted the blade of his pen knife between the door and its frame, managing to catch the locked bolt and escape into the deserted hall.

In the corridor of the empty building, he filled his lungs with delicious air. This would be a good time to call in the police. He had risked his life too often. There were others in a far better position to stop Miss Syn than Winston, and he could maximize the odds of capturing her by calling in help.

"What the hell are you talking about, Tamera?" Winston protested. "I don't need any help!"

She tried to reason with him. "Why take unnecessary chances? You can't expect to win every battle alone, Winston."

"Of course I can." She was really getting on his nerves. "What's the point of being the hero, if you've got to call for help? God, woman, what's the matter with you?"

"There's nothing the matter with me," she said bitterly. "The problem is you want to act like an immature child all the time—"

"Fine," he said and rudely snapped away.

* * *

There were plenty of other channels Winston could SNAP to. Each person in the Vaults received his or her personal transmission from a Guardian Angel. It was a simple matter to SNAP to Gene's channel and eavesdrop on his quiet cabin in the backwoods of Earth's ancient middle-America, or Lena's romantic dreamworld, or Mike's juvenile sexual fancies, or Crystal's strange melodic land of sensory-overload, but none of those experiences fulfilled Winston's yearnings for hard and fast adventure.

He had been an assistant accountant and computer programmer before the GRGA took him, and his fondest wish upon being frozen had been to live the life of an internationally-renowned, independent operative, moving from intrigue to intrigue, always one step ahead of the Law and the Ungodly. Tamera had understood this immediately and her tales of clandestine bio-warfare, high-stakes gambling and breath-taking danger drew Winston into the fantasy world he'd always envied.

That was back years ago at the beginning of their relationship. Today, Winston realized, the old girl was starting to pressure him into other forms of entertainment; tales with devoted and controlled protagonists. But this was <u>his</u> recreation; <u>his</u> time of escape from the complexities of the MARSDAX index. He'd slaved for years as a lowly accountant; this was his time to live the life he'd always dreamed of, not some socially responsible, careful and contemplative life-style of a what? Monk?

But he couldn't deny that he was caught in her siren song; enraptured by the beauty of her narration. He loved Tamera for her kindness, her understanding, and her hopeful expectations that someday a cure would be developed for Winston's illness and he would arise free from his icy prison. Then, they could at last meet and touch and breathe each other's spirit. He knew there could be no "living" without her. Yes, he'd been the demanding, egotistical fool, for turning her off.

Winston Clarke SNAPPED to Tamera's channel and called her name.

* * *

It was a dry and cool Sunday evening when The Bishop decided to pay a casual visit to the newly-opened Roby Art Gallery. The rooms, high atop the Olympus Mons Hotel were filled with an intellectual crowd marveling at the collection of oils, pastels, watercolors, and ceramics.

"Now to truly appreciate the Artist's work," explained the doe-eyed brunette attendant, "you must know a little about woodcuts. Are you familiar with the term?"

Winston smiled. "Early Earth art, if I'm not mistaken."

"Very good!" She wrinkled her pert nose. "The drawing was at first sketched on the surface of a block of wood..."

Winston began speaking word-for-word with his attractive tour guide. "...and the area surrounding the art is cut away, exposing the raised surface to be inked and—Wait just a damn minute," Winston interrupted himself. "Why do I know all of this already?"

Acting as if she hadn't heard Winston's last comment, the girl introduced a tall, blond-bearded man. "Well, if you really like them," she said, "why don't you tell the artist, himself?"

"I know this man," Winston said. "He's Alex—"

"Sir," the girl smiled. "May I introduce Alex Szabo, the artist whose work you've been—"

"NO!" he shouted. "Tamera, you're screwing up again! I've already lived this adventure."

There was no response at first, except the art and its inhabitants were swept away in a blur and Winston was left alone.

* * *

"Winston?"

"Who...who's that?"

"Winston, this is Mr. Simon, Chief Admin of the Christopher Vaults. How are you feeling?"

"Wha...where's Tamera?"

"Uh—well, that's the point of my being here, Winston."

"Why am I living a portion of my life all over again? I don't understand."

"Technically, Winston, it's not 'your life.' Tamera has fabricated these fantasies for you as a reward for your continued efforts in the Corporation's Neuro-electronic programs. I'm sure you're aware that your 'work-time' programs are vital—"

"Never mind that, Simon. Where the hell is Tamera?"

"Tamera's not, uh...available. The current storyline is familiar because we've looped her narrative from a previous presentation and are sending it back to you again, partly because we felt you'd enjoy the experience, and partly because—"

"Because it's cheaper than employing a full-time Angel. I know you, Simon. You're trying to save a few credits at the expense of my sanity. Now, put Tamera back on line!"

Simon was silent for a moment, then: "You are correct. Money is tight, but—"

SNAP.

* * *

Tamera slept fitfully. Her dreams were filled with a young Winston walking arm-in-arm with her on a warm day through a lush, green forest. Rain patted lightly against the leaves and dimpled the surface of a small lake. They crossed an old wooden bridge together, stopping halfway to let the sun-shower wash their faces.

She looked down at the reflection in the water's surface. Winston was dressed in a full military uniform with gold braid and epaulets. Next to him stood a young girl with pale skin, dark eyes, long blonde hair, and a pastel dress with puffed sleeves and a Peter Pan collar.

The image shimmered slightly and the rain increased in strength. It pelted at her now; striking like gravel. She ran and turned and saw Winston running the opposite direction. She started to call to him, but her foot caught on the long, wet dress and she felt herself going over the side of the bridge.

The water rose up and engulfed her, enfolded her, dragging her down to cold darkness.

Tamera's Engagement

* * *

"Winston? Winston, I know you can hear me. You've put us all in a hell of a spot, you know that, don't you? Look, there's no sense keeping it from you any longer. I want you to prepare yourself for a shock. Things cannot be as they were before; Tamera is dying.

"Winston? Do you hear me? She knew it was coming, Winston. She developed a rare form of GRGA and she's, well, she's getting along in years now. Remember that week I had to talk to you while she was in the hospital? Well, I'm afraid the operation wasn't successful. There's nothing more we can do."

Winston fought to control his emotions. "Put her on. I want to talk to her."

"Listen, Winston, you can't let this bother you. You can depend on us. We won't let you down. We need your data management skills, and we're preparing a new Angel for you beginning tomorrow."

"I don't want a new Angel."

"Ah...I don't think you understand. We know the shock is—"

"I don't want a new Angel. Put Tamera into the system, Simon. Freeze her like I am and arrange a way for me to be able to snap to her."

"Uh...I don't think that's possible, besides

I'm not certain she wants to...Well, I'm sure the new girl—"

"DO IT, SIMON, OR YOU WILL NEVER GET CO-OPERATION FROM ME AGAIN."

"But think of the potential risk. The danger to both—"

SNAP

* * *

Tamera felt the tears gathering in her eyes. "I don't know. I— I can't..."

"Why are you so paranoid, woman? I haven't suffered any ill effects. Simon will find a way to connect our—"

"But two minds in coldsleep merged together? I don't know; it's never been done before."

"You're forgetting something," Winston said. "I've got a personal Guardian Angel."

Tamera didn't laugh. "It's not just the unknown of coldsleep that bothers me," she said. "I don't think I can live the way you do; all those sudden and fantastic adventures. I need more to my life; something constant, calm, and quiet."

Winston wasn't sure what she meant, but he knew that if he lost her, he lost everything. "Your life is over," he pleaded. "What better choice have you, than to join me?"

Tamera's Engagement

Tamera took a deep breath. "I'm afraid, Winston. I...I'm not sure anymore what I want."

"Dammit, woman, you're my whole life! I'm willing to take whatever risk necessary for the chance to be with you. Now, you've got to do likewise. Just say yes, please, and Simon will arrange for your entrance to the Vault. It's our only chance of staying together, darling."

"Oh, Winston..."

"I love you, Tamera. Say yes, and we can be happy forever!"

Those were the words she'd been waiting so long to hear. It was like a promise fulfilled. Her heart raced. Breathlessly, she answered, "Yes, Winston. Oh, yes! I want to be with you."

* * *

There was an instant of severe coldness, and then she woke, feeling strangely light in mind and body. The air seemed cleaner than any she'd ever experienced. Fresher, she thought, as if it had just been born of newly-grown plants.

Was she floating weightless? Where had all the pain gone?

"Tamera?"

That sounded like... "Winston?"

"How are you feeling?"

"I..., Winston, where are you?"

The soft whiteness around her opened and the handsome figure of Winston Clarke stepped through with a casual elegance of a natural-born dancer. "Hallo, old girl," he beamed.

He looked just as she'd often described him; trim, youthful, vibrant with health and assurance. "Winston." His name lingered on her lips.

He laughed slightly and stepped forward with the grace of a cat. "Welcome to my dream, sweetheart. Come; let's have a look at you."

The white mist evaporated silently, exposing an elegant bedroom; the colors and textures unlike anything available on Mars. A wooden, canopied bed with light blue sheets and a spread that matched the window curtains.

An open window! The sight of it froze her for an instant. A beautiful passage to brilliant, warm sunlight; a soft breeze filled with lush, tropical scents and the songs of birds. She turned to him in wonder and caught the flash-image of herself in a full-length mirror.

"You're beautiful," he told her. And it was true.

Tamera's body was that of her twentieth year. She turned slowly from side to side, observing the swell of her form and the glowing waves of her long, blond hair. "How...?"

He took her gently in his arms, gazing

deeply into her eyes. "This is our world, darling; it's made up from your dreams and bits of the stories you've told me over the years. Part cyberspace, part fantasy. But it's ours, and you're with me now." A shadow crossed his features. "Of course, we'll only be able to live the reality that's been previously looped, but—"

"No...No, Winston," she said unsteadily. "I not sure, yet, but, I feel...I feel as though I can still affect the narrative. Maybe we're stronger now that we're together, your dreams blended with mine."

Winston concentrated. "My god! You mean we can...?"

She laughed. It was the musical laugh of her youth and it gave her a wonderful idea. "Let's try an experiment," she said. "You go into the next room and let's see if I can still generate a new reality for you away from me."

He hesitated.

"I'm fine," she said to his unasked question. "I've never felt better. Never more complete. Now, go."

His soft brown eyes held hers with a smile. And then he turned and walked through the open door into the oriental dining room.

* * *

Both men quietly finished their meal and

rose from their cushions at the low table. The reptile guard in the red robe was now lurking in the doorway behind the Bishop.

"I suppose," Winston said, glancing at the bedroom door and feeling a satisfying swell of anticipation, "you want the miniaturized diamonds, now." He withdrew the packet and handed it to his host.

The man poured the sparkling stones into his fat palm. "They are more beautiful than I imagined," said the Chinese, greedily. "But I must not keep you. You will miss your plane."

The Bishop thrust his foot between his host's legs, seized his arm, and grunting under the ponderous weight, flung the man in an ancient ju-jitsu maneuver flat on his back on the floor.

"It's working, Tamera. This is all new to me," he called with delight as the floor trembled under the impact.

But Winston had little chance to feel the thrill. Swift strides brought him to the reptile guard, who, to the Bishop's surprise, hurled up his hands in abject surrender.

"Please, you do not hit me. I was made to help him," the scaly creature babbled.

The fat host rose to his knees. "Why...why you do this?"

"Because, you're not the man I came to see,"

the Bishop said, recovering the packet of gems. "If you observed Chinese custom, you would have known that a host always seats himself with his back to the door. It shows that he is not afraid of sudden attack and provides the guest with the best position in case an enemy forces his way into the house. Obviously, you hid my client somewhere, while you took his place."

Tamera's voice floated in from the bedroom. "Ask them about the basement, darling."

The Oriental's face looked like a goldfish that had just been surprised by a mirror.

"Thank you, Angel," Winston called back. "And now I think I'll do the responsible thing and call the police."

"Wonderful," she called. "I didn't decide to do that; you did. So we share the control of this new reality, after all."

The confused Chinese gave a deep sigh and came to his feet. "Okay, Mr. Clarke," he said. "You win."

"Which is all I've ever wanted," Winston replied.

"Come back in here, darling," Tamera said, "I've a little surprise for you. It's what I've always wanted."

From the bedroom came a sound that made his heart swell; the cry of a sleepy baby.

UNHAPPY TRAILS

It was a single-story, brick-façade house, set back from the road with a gravel drive, surrounded by mature trees. When I got out of my car, climbed the three steps and rang the bell, I was greeted by the familiar yapping of two small dogs rushing the door. They kept it up for almost a half-minute before Dan came and let me in, deadpanning, "Wanna buy a dog?"

I smiled in spite of myself. Dan and I had been friends since we'd met in film class at The Ohio State University thirty years earlier.

He shook my hand strongly and said, "How's it, hero?" Five foot six inches, sandy receding hair, rimless bifocals, easy grin. "Want some coffee?"

The twin miniature Beagle pups were a pair of oxfords with twitching tails, sniffing and wetting my shoes with their noses. We all moved as a unit through the kitchen and into the sunroom where Dan kept his currently favorite books, movies and pipes. I noticed a dozen or so Roy Rogers and Hopalong Cassidy DVDs stacked neatly beside the TV.

It was a warm day in late autumn and I had

come bearing a birthday gift.

The ex-chief of police and I shared a love of old movies and older detective stories. This year, I brought him a first edition of the movie version of Hammett's *The Glass Key*; the one with Alan Ladd and Veronica Lake on the dust jacket.

Taking the book out of the brown paper bag I had used as gift wrap, he nodded. "This is great, Scotty. I've always enjoyed it."

I nodded, too. "I went back and re-watched the 1942 version of the film. My favorite scene is where Ladd confronts a guy and they argue eye to eye. Then, instead of throwing a punch, Ladd merely kicks the guy in the shin, causing him to hop around on one leg while Ladd calmly walks away."

"That's one of my favorite bits, too," Dan chuckled. "Maybe they should have called the movie *The Glass Knee.*"

"Ouch," I winced and fake-limped over to an easy chair. I continued to rub my knee as if in pain.

Dan watched and selected a pipe from a nearby rack. "Which reminds me, are you still going on those long walks in the park?"

I gazed out the window at a stand of pines across the lake. A couple of Canada geese flew overhead. "These days, being out on trail is my best remedy for clearing away stress from pounding the keyboard at the paper. You should try it," I advised. "In fact, something interesting happened while I was out at Slate Run Metro Park last week doing a 6-miler."

"Go ahead," Dan said, waving out the kitchen match and leaning back in his chair. "Spin me your usual rambling yarn."

I cleared my throat to get a running start. "Well, the terrain is heavily forested, see, with small open meadows carpeted with wild clover, topped with a cloud-flecked sky. The gravel and dirt trail slants between wooded cliffs, folding back to a burbling creek below."

"Sounds literate."

"Don't interrupt. I had trekked at a steady pace for close to two miles and came out of deep woods into an open prairie where park administrators have built a playground beside a small man-made lake. About twenty paces in front of me, a big, blocky guy with a thin mustache, wearing a dark blue jacket, had two big dogs on separate leashes, walking them through the grass and wildflowers. They were milling around midway between me and the lake. I automatically switched course, of course."

"Too literate," he puffed.

"Okay, so I veered to my right to avoid them;

you happy? But the dogs had seen me now or caught my scent and one of them broke from his leash and dashed top speed directly for me." I paused for dramatic effect and sipped strong coffee from a World's-Best-Police-Officer mug. "He probably weighed over 100 pounds, but came at me like an arrow. Sort of a cross between a wolf hound and a German shepherd with big teeth, burning eyes and red diamond patch of fur on his forehead."

"Not teeth," Dan said. "Fangs."

"Yeah, well, so I brought up my hiking staff to defend myself, while the guy in the blue jacket hollered and struggled to hold back the other excited dog. I tried to decide between standing my ground or running across the open field, when the guy yelled, 'Heel! Heel, Lucky!' And the dog stopped dead on command, but continued to growl and stare at me with determined hate."

"Lucky?"

"Yeah, apparently that's the dog's name. So the blocky guy caught up to Lucky and we all stood there breathing hard, men and dogs, just as a Park Ranger cruised by in his truck, making regular rounds."

Dan went "Hmmm".

I reached down and rubbed one of the pups behind the ear. Of course, the other one wanted it too. "Well, the blocky guy was restless, moving from foot to foot. He buried his tanned face deep in his beard and said, 'I'll give you $100 not to say anything to the Ranger.' The dogs stayed quiet and the Blocky Guy pulled a smartphone from his jacket pocket and held up in my direction.

"*No real harm done*, I thought, right? So I swallowed and waved to the passing truck and the Ranger waved back and Blocky waved back and the Ranger slowly drove down the road and out of sight.

"Blocky reached into his back pocket and pulled out a worn brown wallet, but I told him, 'Don't worry about it,' and walked back out of the field and into the woods. But the more I thought about it, the more I wondered why he would offer as much as $100, not to alert the park authorities.

"So I turned around and walked back to where I was still hidden by the brush and watched him load the dogs into the white van and slowly drive away.

"It all seemed perfectly normal, but what the heck, I made a note of the license plate: EA78NG. And that was that."

My coffee was cold. Dan picked up a pencil and wrote on the brown paper bag that I'd given him. "When was this again?"

"Last Monday afternoon, when it was cool and dry. Perfect weather for hiking."

"Is that why you came here today? To share your latest saga?"

"No," I protested. "I came here to celebrate your, what, eightieth birthday, Old Cop."

It was his turn to wince. "Sixty-sixth," he said. "You were at Slate Run Park, right? I wonder if you know that the next day there was an escape from the level three security facility near there."

"No kidding...."

"The Chief of Security is a friend and keeps me notified of events."

"No kidding...."

"The escapee has not been found. For some reason, the guard dogs couldn't track him."

"Can you check with your friend and see if they have a dog with a red diamond on its forehead?"

"Maybe tomorrow. Today's my birthday." He put down his pipe and came to his feet. "And I just happen to have a DVD of *The Glass Key*. You might get a kick out of it."

"Ouch," I winced again. "Sounds fun."

* * *

"Sounds dull," my editor said. "Besides, I need you back on the Political beat."

"But, he can get me inside, Andrea. And he even knows the Chief of Security."

She pushed a strand of hair from her face and squinted at me. "Sounds weak, too," she said, starting to walk away. "You've got better things to do."

"Come on," I followed. "We haven't published a prison tour in ages and we've *never* done a blog from behind bars before. It'll get us lots of comments and re-twits on our webpage."

I'd been with the *Columbus Inquirer* for over eleven years and watched it slowly shrink and go "social". I wasn't the best journalist on staff, but I was the most loyal to the traditions of a classic reporter. Still, I'd gradually started to learn how to blog and hoot and post stories to our Facebook page.

She turned back to scowl at me. *Must have forgotten to put her contacts in today.* "I know that you know that it's not 're-twits', Scotty. And you're not going to be able to coast on your involvement in the *Just Sweats* murder forever."

"Still... I'd like to take a crack at it."

"You're like a dog with a bone. Once you get the scent...."

* * *

Dan drove us in his Ford 150 through the

cool, grey morning past Grove City to the Bolton Correctional Institution.

I saw randomly stacked chunks of grey concrete with a white colonial façade entrance. Level 1 inmates had placed painted, white rocks along the drive. A high chain-link fence with three Yield signs rolled to the right on stubby wheels to let Dan's truck into the visitor's lot.

There were cameras mounted on the corners of the building and above the solid grey entrance door. Dan talked to the video screen and showed his creds. We were buzzed through the sally port double set of doors to a holding area. All very cold and official.

I emptied my pockets into a grey tub on a conveyor belt that led to an x-ray machine, like the ones they have at the airport. A prison officer who looked like a linebacker bagged my stuff and waved a metal detector hoop up and down my arms, legs and torso.

The windowless room was brightly lit from a cascade of florescent panels overhead. The concrete walls gleamed with grey paint. More cameras high in every corner. Low 'locker-room' benches bolted to the polished grey and white tile floor. Intake holding rooms. All very official and cold.

The Desk Officer listened while Dan told him

why we were there, and then made a call. Ten minutes later, we were greeted by Deputy of Operations Jerry Conner who'd already been briefed of our visit. He shook Dan's hand and looked at me with an open expression. "You the reporter?"

"Journalist." I shook his warm hand. "Scott Robinson."

"And you think?" He let it hang there.

I glanced at Dan and then said, "I think I may know something about the guy who escaped last week."

Deputy Conner rattled off: "Bolton Correctional seeks to provide offenders of felony convictions within the State of Ohio a safe, efficient, humane and appropriately secure correctional...."

"Yeah, I saw that on your website."

I watched him study me. "You don't make friends very quickly, do you?"

There was nothing to say to that. But I went ahead anyway. "I've done my homework and the guy who got away was Omar Aldagon, who was in here for making threats against the federal government, according to the state attorney general's office. How exactly did he get away?"

Conner glared at me with a stare that was hard enough to crack diamonds. It wasn't my most shining hour. Dan quickly stepped in, saying, "Look, Jerry. What Mr. Robinson here means is that we think we know something about how Aldagon got away. But first, can you tell us how he got beyond your confines?"

Conner addressed Dan, as if I'd faded away. "He hid up above the air ducts during the afternoon and got out when the gates were opened to receive a returning work crew. We tracked him, but couldn't run him to ground."

"Did you track him with the dogs?" Dan asked.

"Of course."

"Including Lucky?"

"Among others, yes."

"Who handles Lucky now?"

Conner considered. "That would be Officer Crandall."

"Blocky guy with an anemic mustache? We think that he tampered with the dog's training and that's why you couldn't track him."

I watched Conner process this. There were nests of wrinkles at the edges of his eyes and hard lines at the sides of his mouth. "How do you know Crandall?"

I answered by relating my encounter with Lucky and Company at the park.

The lines at his mouth got deeper and the muscles at his jaw swelled. "I cannot act without evidence, you understand," he said. "But I can take steps to ensure the security of the facility while we investigate." He stepped behind his desk and punched a button on his phone. "Have Officer Crandall put on unpaid leave immediately and escorted off the premises."

Cold. Official.

"Satisfied?"

I was impressed and a little embarrassed. "Do I still get the tour?"

* * *

On the drive back, Dan said, "I promised him that you wouldn't publish anything on this yet."

"What? Why?"

"I talked with Conner while you were being shown around. He kicked Crandall out, hoping to trail him and possibly lead them back to Aldagon."

He had seemed to jump on it pretty quickly.

Sunlight glared off Dan's glasses. "Conner says that lately Crandall has been ranting about how prison life is soft with free medical, dental, three squares and easy access to the Internet. Called it a bed and breakfast. He's even mentioned something about the Foundation Citizens."

"The right-wing supremacist group? They were involved with the shooting of a prison director in Colorado a few months ago."

"I know. You can see why Conner doesn't want you to print anything yet. Everything I'm telling you now is off the record."

"Yeah but, these Foundationers are essentially domestic terrorists. There was that backpack bomb with the fishing weights coated with rat poison in Spokane in 2011 and the gallon of napalm wired to a suburban home up in Cleveland the year before. Dan, you can't expect me to suppress this."

"You don't have any evidence," Dan said. "Just the hearsay story that I'm telling you now."

"Yeah but...."

"Yeah but, yourself, Scotty. I promised that you'd sit on it for a couple of days, so Conner and his people can work the problem. I did you a favor getting you inside. Don't make me go back on my word." The road ahead of us was clear, so he glanced my way. "And you need to work on improving your people skills and stop being such a loner."

I knew he was right, but I still made a sound in my throat like I'd swallowed a tack.

* * *

The next day, back in the office, I worked on an election year politics story about Alex Newton, state senate candidate from the heart of the heartland, who was scheduled to smile and wave during next week's OSU vs. Michigan football game. I knew him for being a firebrand lawyer with a head full of graying hair and a mouthful of expensive dental work. A pro at slapping babies and kissing backs. He was supported by several of the unions for his stance on the homeless problem and the Green party for being anti-fracking. Nobody really cared much about Newton, but politics and sports is what the news is all about, sometimes.

I'd saved a draft of the story on my laptop and went to get a fresh cup of Dark French Roast from the Gevalia machine in the break room. It had been awhile since I'd contributed to the Community Coffee Fund, so I folded a twenty and dropped it into the jar, when a local news story on the overhead TV monitor told the public that a car had gone off the road, through a guard rail and landed upside down at the bottom of Marblecliff quarry. The driver, one Edmond Crandall, had been crushed flat by the impact and "died instantly", if you could believe the local TV news nerds. They had no idea what the real story was. I wasn't sure I did either.

I called Dan about Crandall's death. He said the authorities were working on it and I should continue to hold my water. *Damn.*

That night, I dined alone on pinot grigio and frozen pizza, watched *The Big Lebowski* and took my headache off to bed. As I slipped into a restless sleep, I thought, *Screw 'em, I'm taking myself out on trail tomorrow, so this dude can abide.*

* * *

Wednesday was supposed to warm up fast into the high eighties. I decided to get an early start. Dressed in khakis, sturdy shoes, a denim shirt and my multi-pocketed, light-weight fishing vest, I pulled my rust bucket into the empty lot at Pickerington Ponds Metro Park. The lavender light was just spreading across the sky, diffusing the darkness, while the eastern horizon began to glow like the mouth of a furnace.

I had the place all to myself. It's one of the flattest and quietest parks in Central Ohio. The morning air was cool and smelled of damp earth. The trail was crushed gravel and wound through a collection of old farm pastures that had been combined and flooded to create a seventeen acre wetlands with runoffs filled with cattails and shoulder-high tufts of wild grass. As I crunched along the winding path, my spirit lifted and my mind began to float free.

Being on trail is cathartic for me. I think about things I'd done wrong and the things I'd done right. Where I'd chosen correctly and where I'd gone wrong. I had chosen to follow the safe and successful route of being a general news reporter, instead of a novelist. As a result, it often felt like I'd given away my unique perspective, in exchange for the common man's POV; the universal man who gets a weekly paycheck, who reads the daily newspaper and then discards it.

But, whatever was lacking in my life—whatever I thought I'd lost—I always hoped that I'd find it hidden on trail. Something about being true to the basic principles or Curley's "One Thing" that could make me a better person. Dumb stuff, like that.

I hiked for over an hour, clearing my mind and looping along the trail that circled Arrowhead Marsh, watching the egrets stretch their wings in the sun, finally yo-yoing back to the public parking lot where a green SUV was now parked next to my car.

As I strolled nearer, two guys got out of the other car and one of them pointed a sweaty, stern face and gun at me, saying, "Keep quiet and give me your keys."

The rest of our conversation was even shorter and so was the trip, with me at gunpoint in my own passenger seat and the SUV following, until we all bounced up a long driveway to an old farm house with a dilapidated For Sale sign out at the highway in front of a 30-acre lot that hadn't been plowed for at least two years.

* * *

Maybe it was the adrenalin from the danger, but I was pissed. I struggled to keep myself under control. They helped with their guns.

We parked next to the white van that they had used to transport the dogs and trudged up the three sagging steps to the front porch. "Bring him on in," I heard a voice call through the screen door.

Inside the house stood a guy with stern brows and faint flame tattoos rising from under the collar of his open shirt. "Omar Aldagon," he said and stuck out his right hand for me to shake. When I reach for it, he slaps me hard. "Asshole."

The left side of my face stung and I felt hot with embarrassment. "Is that your official title?"

He tilted his head to the side, like a hound.

His shoulders are narrow and he has stiff, black hair that no amount of grease seemed capable of flattening. He blew out a laugh and had his men turn out my pockets, leaving me with my comb, handkerchief, pen, pad, loose change and wallet. He took my phone and held it up. "These are a godsend." He hit me hard in the shoulder with his open hand. "That's how we found you."

They had traced me from a biometric scan app when my photo was taken in the park via Crandall's smartphone. And they had a contact with access to DMV info, who used some software to match the photo with the one on my driver's license. *Nobody is off-the-grid any more. Technology can get to anyone.*

I put it out there. "You murdered Crandall."

"Yes," Aldagon grinned with yellow teeth. "We didn't need that butt crack anymore, but we do need you."

"To do what?"

"To report the facts of the big story after the big event."

I noticed a bunch of candidate posters and flyers for Newton's campaign stacked up in the corners of the main room of the farm house. These guys appeared to be supporting Newton's political campaign for the state senate, but I knew they had something to do with the

Foundation Citizens. *So why do they want me to believe that they are part of Newton's support team?*

Aldagon's lips were compressed; his neck muscles bunched. "You're going to be our guest here for a few days and when you wake up late Sunday, you'll be ready to tell our exclusive, inside story."

That sounded like I'd do well to bide my time until they let me go. *But why Sunday?* It slowly dawned on me that Aldagon's big event might have a political angle. He and the Foundationers intended to do something on Saturday and blame it on Newton, based on my reporting. They planned to use me to make people believe that Newton is responsible for.... The words *bomb* and *football game* made an 80-point headline in my head.

* * *

They kept me locked in a windowless room and fed me microwaved Chicken Alfredo packs. The water bottles had already been opened. I figured that they were feeding me small portions of a sedative over time, so it would be easy to fully drug me unconscious on Friday, while they're setting up the "big event".

I've had experience during long hikes of going without food or water, so I scooped the food from the cardboard containers and piled it on the top shelf of an empty closet. I poured the water down a crack in the floor behind my squeaking bunk. I hoped the flies and ants didn't give me away.

By Friday, I was acting doped, which wasn't hard, since I hadn't eaten in days. I try to stay alert as Aldagon comes into the room with a syringe and stops.

There is a knock at the front door of the farm house. Faintly, I hear Dan's apologetic voice. His car broke down? No bars on his cell? Can he use the phone? *He wrote the license plate number on the birthday wrapping.*

Then, lots of other voices; all shouting. Thumping. Firing. "Show us your hands!"

Aldagon's eyes looked like nails driven into his face. He yanks me out of the room, toward the back door, gun to my neck. "Okay, shithead. Move your ass."

I stumble and he pulls me up. We're face to face and it comes to me to kick him in the shin, just like Alan Ladd in *The Glass Key*. He yelps and automatically grabs for his leg.

Behind me, Dan yells, "Scotty, get down."

* * *

There's no way of knowing how many lives were saved that day. The Foundationers planned to set off several explosive devices at the packed football stadium, but they were stopped.

And with only one casualty.

"You do the best you can," Dan told me from his bed at the hospital. "And if things don't work out, you let them go."

When I'm back out on trail again, I won't be alone. There'll be two yapping dogs with me, sniffing and searching forever for the Old Cop.

THE BORIS KILLOFF

It was the summer of 1938. I was sitting in my office on Fulton Street, catching up on my foot dangling while sniffing the faint aroma of fish that drifted through the bullet-scarred window behind me. A client opened the pebbled-glass door and shuffled in. He a tall, lean guy in his late forties with deep, penetrating eyes and a deep, penetrating voice.

"Someone is trying to kill me," he said, removing his gray Homburg and patting the line it had left across his forehead with a snow-white linen handkerchief. He looked good in tones of black and white, but the line across his brow reminded me of something...sinister.

I hefted my heels off the desk top and struck a kitchen match to a gasper. "You're that guy," I said, fanning the air with my palm. "That Frankenstein guy!"

"Please," he moaned in a slight lisp. "That's all I ever hear and I'd rather not discuss it, now. I'm in desperate need of a reliable detective and I've heard that you fit the bill. Help me and I'll pay you one hundred dollars a day."

"That's a lot of jack, Jack. What kind of help

do you want?"

"I need to stop the man who's threatening me."

Blackmail, I thought. But who'd have anything on *this* guy? "Look, Mr.—"

"Kaye," he supplied, sitting in the rickety client chair. "William Henry Kaye."

"Look, Mr. Kaye, if I'm going to help you, I'm going to need a little background information. Who is this guy you're talking about and why is he after you?"

His eyes got misty as his gaze followed the rising line of my cigarette smoke to the slowly-revolving ceiling fan. "It all began," he said, and I reached for the bottle of Rye I kept tucked in my battered desk for use whenever I felt a flashback coming on, "thirty years ago in London, England...."

* * *

We dodged the traffic on Baker Street in fog as thick as hasty pudding. "Strike me pink, Gov," I said, tugging at one of my drooping stockings. "'Ow ever did you figure it out?"

"Rudimentary deduction, Willy," replied the thin, hawkish man, as he bent to place a sovereign in my grimy hand. "The Professor once published a monograph on the Dynamics of an Asteroid. This, coupled with the information you've just related to me about his recent visits to the Royal Astronomical Society, leads to only one inescapable conclusion. He is planning something that could quite possibly have earth-shattering consequences, and we must hurry, if we're to stop him."

We hailed a cab and set off for the Society's observatory, north of Hyde Park.

I had begun working for the Great Detective several months earlier, having run away from my home in Dulwich. While searching the East End for some kind of theatrical work, I'd encountered stories of this strange man who had a penchant for acting and mysteries. He and a physician friend soon made me an honorary Irregular of their private police force.

"The Professor is an arcane man," my employer instructed as we stepped down from our cab ride. "He will stop at nothing to—"

Suddenly, a bright, bluish light beamed heavenward from behind the dark edifice of the observatory. "Quick, Willy," the detective said, dashing into the night. "He's engaged the device."

"What device?" I asked, but my companion was gone.

When I caught up with him, he was locked in a struggle with his insane enemy. They were clutching each other in a terrible death grip as a huge mechanical contraption steamed and pulsed and emitted its eerie beam skyward.

"Quick, Willy," the Detective cried over his shoulder. "Pull that lever!"

I glanced at the hissing device that threatened to destroy one end of the observatory's basement. There was a control lever mounted in the floor.

The Professor screamed in a high, crackling voice, "Nooo! The planet must be destroyed!"

I grasped the lever and looked to my mentor. His eyes locked on mine and I pulled back on the lever as if it were a hand brake on the Dover Special. Instantly, the room was aflame. The earth shook and I stumbled to reach my companion.

"You fools," cried the Professor. "I've waited thirty years and now you've destroyed my chance to contact them."

Through the bellowing oily smoke, the Detective's hands lifted me and I heard him say, "Quick, Willy. We must escape. The place is an inferno."

"But, the Professor..." I cried as we exited into the chilled, night air.

The building exploded with the force of a thousand cannons. We buried our faces in the wet grass as the debris fell all around us. Finally, rising and dusting his Inverness coat with his palms, my employer enjoined me to return with him to his lodgings where we might relate our adventures to his medical friend.

* * *

The room seemed to be spinning. I steadied myself by knocking back another shot of rye and said, "I don't get it, pal. Who was this Professor? And why was he trying to blow up the world?"

My client looked at me with a patented, raised eyebrow I had seen in many a strange flick. "I'm afraid it wasn't this world he was trying to destroy, but another in a far distant star system."

"That's all, brother," I said, slamming the flat of my hand on the top of my desk. "You're loonier than a Warner Brothers cartoon. I want you out of here, right now."

"But he's trying to kill me," the old guy protested, coming to his feet. "Don't you see? It's been thirty years and the configuration of the stars is again in alignment. I'm the only one who can stop him; the only one who knows."

"Look, Doc," I said, coming around the side of the desk, "I'm going to configure your stars for you, if you don't get—"

He came straight at me, saying, "But you've got to believe me!" And then I heard the shot and he fell into my arms.

I saw a gloved hand throw the pistol onto the floor of my office from the half-opened door. I wanted to make a dash for the hall, but by the time I got untangled from the clutches of my dying client, the killer was gone.

"Palomar," the old guy gasped, when I came back to lift him to the couch. "His new laboratory is hidden under...."

The actor went limp in my hands. The blood from the wound in his back was cupped in my palm. I looked at his blank, glazed eyes and said, "Okay, Doc, you just hired yourself a detective."

* * *

One week later, I stepped off the Twentieth Century Limited in downtown Los Angeles. It was so hot I thought about ditching my kitchen matches; I didn't want anything to ignite spontaneously. I was already sizzling hot for lamming out of town with a dead actor in my office. I'd figured the safest way to clear myself was to head west and find the killer. It also put a lot of distance between me and the nosey New York coppers.

I bought a used 1930 Chevrolet Six Coupe from some mad man for two hundred smackers, which pretty much wiped out the last of my income from the sale of my saloon back East. Six months ago, my partner had been rubbed out by the mob in a fight over the management of that joint. That's when I decided to stick my neck out and into the detective business in order to track down his killer. It had been one hell of an adventure, but that, as they say, is another story.

The roads south to Mount Palomar were rough, dry and dusty. I passed the time listening to the car's radio. Fred Allen was ribbing Jack Benny and the Shadow was clouding the mind of a guy called the Creeper. I love high drama.

It was dusk when I pulled around the final curve of the mountain road and came to a stop outside the main observatory building. Its solid round mass rose above me in the star spangled sky. I'd called ahead from the City of Angels, telling a female voice that I was a reporter with the *Trib*. Now, all I had to do was act the part, until I could get a line on the actor's killer.

Straightening my hat and tie, I rapped my knuckles against the front door, and it opened.

Her negligee smacked my eyes and her perfume KO'ed my nose. The nightie was black chiffon, three degrees thinner than a silkworm's breath. It frothed around her in diaphanous folds, hinting at what it concealed and concealing extremely little. My pants were getting excited. I tried sucking a breath between my teeth and then realized my mouth was wide open. Finally, I asked, "Is the Professor in?"

She laughed in a high musical scale that reminded me of porcelain wind chimes. "There are no professors here, I think. Are you the gentleman from the newspaper?"

"Yeah," I mumbled. "Say, aren't you afraid of catching cold in that outfit?"

She waved her long, dark lashes at me and pouted. And that's when a ton of lead came down on the back of my head and knocked out my lights.

I was swimming in the vastness of space, watching planets form and stars explode. It was a pretty good show, except that somebody ruined it by dumping the Milky Way in my face.

I sputtered and coughed and tried to sit up. My hands and feet were tied with rough, heavy cord.

"Sooo," hissed a voice, "you are with us again, at last."

The room was full of shadows and steam. Off in the distance, I could make out a figure in a wheelchair against the glowing lights of a control panel that Buck Rogers would have hocked his raygun for.

"The Professor," I mumbled, and the figure wheeled itself forward.

"Yesss," he hissed, his incredibly wrinkled head osculated back and forth like a lizard's. "It was the mention of the word 'professor' that gave you away, my friend. No individual has called me that in years. But I know who sent you. It was that damnable detective. Where is he?"

It seemed to me that, over the years, the good Professor had not experimented with a fully-charged battery. Some of his electrodes must have been rusty. I decided to try and out-bluff him.

"We've known about your plans to blow up the earth for a long time, Professor. You didn't have to kill that man in New York."

"Ha, ha! You fool," he shouted, turning a dial on the control panel. A dull hum came from beneath our feet. "It isn't the earth I plan to destroy. My infernal device harnesses waves of gravity and focuses them through the 200 foot optical lenses of the telescope, sending them to a distant planet where another scientist will send down –"

"Whoa, Doc," I shouted. "Hold the phone. Am I supposed to believe that you've had conversations with a gent from another planet?"

The humming grew louder. Sparks began erupting from behind one of the electrical dodads.

"The emissary will follow the gravity waves back this location and I will be his Master. He will have powers and abilities far beyond those of mortal men. He will be able to leap tall buildings in a single bound, bend steel in his bare hands, and—"

The Professor ranted on and on, saliva gathering at the corners of his mouth. The room was filling with smoke and steam, looking like it might blow any minute. I struggled at the ropes that bound hands, while the Professor continued to rave.

"—will fight a never-ending battle for greed, injustice and the criminal way," he panted.

"I think not, Professor," another voice rang out from the shadows. And in the dim light, I could see another figure—this one, lean and determined—advancing on the Professor from out of the mists.

"You're alive!" the Professor screamed, turning and drawing a sword from somewhere within his wheelchair. "I knew I'd draw you out!"

"Just as I drew you out by sending my faithful Irregular to this New York private detective. I knew you had my man watched, but I never thought you'd stoop to murdering him."

Cool, thin fingers begin to free my bonds. Turning my head, I saw the girl in the black negligee. "Hurry," she urged. "Father will kill him."

The two combatants continued to tumble in and out of the mist. "Which one is your father?" I shouted over the deafening hum. The room was vibrating with the sound of grinding continents.

I picked up the girl and dashed for the door, but a voice from behind us implored, "The lever. The leeever!"

Without a moment's hesitation, the girl jumped from my arms, crying, "Papa," and dove back through the billowing smoke as a wall of stone came crashing down, sealing the three of them in their bizarre tomb forever.

* * *

After that, there wasn't much else for me to do. The world was safe from the threat of whatever the hell the Professor had contacted, but I'd always miss that negligee.

I took it on the lam again, and was never successful in clearing name. Eventually, I got out of the country and the detective racket all together.

So, now I'm just a humble saloon keeper in Paris. A lot of us expatriates have found a home over here. And so have the Germans. But, I don't worry about that. The problems of the world don't amount to a hill of beans to me, now that I've met Ilsa.

(Originally appeared in *Tales of the Unanticipated,* Winter/Spring/Summer, 1991)

ALSO BY JOHN HEGENBERGER

SPYFALL
In October 1959, someone is out for revenge against young L.A. PI, Stan Wade, who has solved a few cases for his main client, Walt Disney. When a CIA agent mistakenly dies in Stan's place, Stan initiates a revenge investigation that leads him outside the country, and his own comfort zone, to stop a nuclear threat to Europe that will remain classified until 2012.

STARFALL
After rescuing Annette Funicello's stand-in from the amorous clutches of Guy Williams, Stan Wade, young, LA-based PI, gets a new, but secret, assignment from his number-one client, Walt Disney. The elder cartoonist and filmmaker wants Stan to investigate a death at Edwards Air Force Base. The victim, who drowned while testing an outer-space uniform, was the eighth astronaut candidate for America's new space agency, NASA. Working out of his cramped office in the back of the Brown Derby restaurant where he's employed as a part-time "bouncer," Stan uncovers much more than a suspicious death...putting his own life—and the lives of those closest to him—in danger.

SPADEFALL
It's 1950, and Stan Wade, L.A. PI, is working on his first case: recovering the stolen manuscript of a

new Sam Spade novel by Dashiell Hammett. This epic hunt will last for a decade, and before it's over will involve Humphrey Bogart, Eleanor Roosevelt, Alfred Hitchcock, Mickey Cohen, Robert Bloch, stripper Candy Barr, and a sleazy nightclub owner named Jack Ruby. Will Stan survive to put all the pieces of this crazy-quilt case together?

It's bullets, volcanoes, espionage, romance, humor, double-crosses, and pop culture references galore as Stan Wade races through another fast-moving, action-packed caper. John Hegenberger's SPADEFALL is the latest entry in one of the best new private series in years and pure reading entertainment. Trying to keep up with Stan Wade is some of the most fun you'll ever have in the pages of a book!

"If you're looking for non-stop action, along with some humor and surprising twists, give this a try." – Bill Crider on SPYFALL, the first book in the Stan Wade series.

<u>CROSS EXAMINATIONS: CRIME IN COLUMBUS</u>
A series of serious crimes: Kidnapping. Murder. Art Thief. Blackmail. Comic Books. "...fast-moving, atmospheric, and consistently surprising..."

Private Investigator Eliot Cross faces heartache, headache, backache, and a royal pain in the neck in these rollicking noir stores from the heart of the Heartland.

JOHN HEGENBERGER

Cross Examinations, Inc. established in 1988

TRIPL3 CROSS
It's 1988, and small-town P.I. Eliot Cross is searching for his long-lost father. Then, a CIA informant says that Dad has been in deep cover for over twenty years. Now, the informant's been murdered and Eliot is on the run.

Scrambling to clear his name, Eliot journeys from Washington D.C. to Havana, Cuba, struggling against deadly drug-runners, syndicate hit-men and his own violent nature. But the worst is yet to come, as Eliot discovers his father is at the center of an international conspiracy, a nuclear threat and a double cross...or is that a triple cross?

Veteran author John Hegenberger spins a yarn that is both an exciting thriller and a compelling piece of "noirstalgia", expertly recreating a sense of late-Eighties paranoia and double-dealing and painting a vivid picture of Washington and Cuba during that era, as well as saving a shocking twist for the very end. TRIPL3 CROSS is pure reading entertainment.

CROSSFIRE
A vanishing corpse...a clout on the head...industrial espionage with millions of dollars at stake...an international conspiracy that threatens the 1988 Summer Olympics...These are just some of the

problems private investigator Eliot Cross has to untangle in CROSSFIRE: THE SCALES OF JUSTICE, the newest novel from popular author John Hegenberger. Fast-paced, filled with mystery, action, and humor, CROSSFIRE is a private eye yarn in the classic mold and a sure bet for entertainment.

MUTINY ON OUTSTATION ZORI
Who stole the space station?

At the far reaches of the Imperium, something's gone terribly wrong on Outstation Zori. The station has cut itself off from all communication, and the corporation that owns it sends a team of specialists to get to the bottom of this mystery. But a young con-man, a rebel leader, and a greedy space pirate are in for a mind-bending shock as they face off against alien races, bizarre religions, and an ultimate betrayal by one of their own.

MUTINY ON OUTSTATION ZORI: A space adventure caper with philosophical overtones.

THE LAST MARTIAN CHRONICLES
From the cold, rocky surface of Mars to the vast reaches of deep space, from the dusty pages of the pulps to the cutting edge medical technology of the future, the stories in John Hegenberger's THE LAST MARTIAN CHRONICLES span the frontiers of science fiction, fantasy, and horror. Unlikely friends

try to survive the dangers of future war in "Keys to the Kingdom". A bizarre fate befalls a famous author in the alternate history story "Howard's Toe". Sinister forces are on the prowl in "Dead Dames in Dayton". Alien visitors come to Earth with surprising results in "Last Contact". And two races face a poignant destiny in "The Last Martian". These stories and others from popular author John Hegenberger are filled with imagination, ingenuity, and heart.

Made in the USA
Charleston, SC
09 May 2016